The Earl of Smu

By

Kate Carteret

ACKNOWLEDGEMENTS

Published by : Dashing Dandies Publishing

Editor : Elizabeth Williams Alareon Media LLC

"If you wake at midnight, and hear a horse's feet,
Don't go drawing back the blind, or looking in the street,
Them that asks no questions they isn't told a lie.
Watch the wall, my darling, while the Gentlemen go by!

Five-and-twenty ponies, trotting through the dark—
With brandy for the Parson and 'baccy for the Clerk.
Laces for a lady and letters for a spy,
And watch the wall, my darling, while the Gentlemen go by!"

A Smuggler's Song by Rudyard Kipling

Chapter One

"Try to take a little water, Lord Northcott, you must. You have not taken a drop since yesterday and Dr Morton said it will do you no good at all to let your body run dry," Clarissa said in a tone she hoped was a little more forceful than she would ordinarily use on the Earl of Northcott.

He was a stubborn man and a most awkward patient in any sickness, but this sickness was worse than anything she had seen him suffer before.

"Dr Morton is too young to be a real doctor, Clarissa. Have you seen his face? Barely a hair upon that chin of his. And his accent is very Cornish, my dear," he finished, as if the last were the greatest of the young doctor's crimes.

"Well, he *is* Cornish, Lord Northcott. As am I. As are you." She held his gaze but noted how pale his eyes were, how muted the brown of the irises.

"You have an answer for everything, Clarissa," he said and choked a little as he began to laugh. "Just like your father always did. Although it is with the Lord's grace that you look like your mother, for you would have been ill-favoured indeed. My goodness, just imagine if you looked like dear old Edmund! I always marvelled at the beauty of his wife. How on earth did he do it?"

"This is procrastination, My Lord!" Clarissa said and poured water from the carafe on the bedside table with exaggerated movements. "Please," she added in a wheedling tone which made the old Earl smile.

"You will always have your way, my dear. Well, let me force it down," he said and tipped his head back enough for Clarissa to gently press the glass to his lips.

He took a little water, perhaps too little for her liking, but Clarissa could see how it exhausted him. She set the glass down on the table and pulled her chair a little closer to the bed. Lord Northcott was breathing hard, as if he had run for a mile and not simply taken a few sips of water. It made her heart ache to see that great bear of a man laid so low, even though signs of his once mighty frame were still in evidence.

She tried to remember when his face hadn't looked so grey and his eyes so faded and realised her guardian had been failing for some time. Just bit by bit, but they were now reaching the crisis, she was sure of it. Worse still, she couldn't rid herself of the feeling that this crisis would turn out to be his last.

Clarissa Tate had only lived at Northcott Hall for the three years since her father had died. The Earl of Northcott and Sir Edmund Tate had been great friends, if a little distant at times, and when her mother had died so many years before, her father had extracted a promise from the Earl that he would watch over his only child if anything happened to him.

Although Clarissa had often wondered if Lord Northcott regretted that hastily made promise, she had never seen any sign of it. She had become something of a companion to him since she'd arrived, often spending the time that she thought either or both of his sons ought to have spared for him.

Clarissa could see that he was now sleeping, although it was not entirely peaceful. She could see that beads of perspiration had broken out across his furrowed brow and she rose again, taking a cool cloth from the bowl on the table and wringing it out before gently applying it to the Earl's forehead. He hardly moved as she dabbed at him with the cloth, cooling him so that he might finally enjoy a more peaceful and restorative slumber.

Clarissa had never been able to fathom the characters of the Earl's sons. Philip Ravenswood, the eldest and the heir to the estate, was a very different man from his father. He was as aloof as his father was approachable, and as proud and arrogant as his father was open-hearted. But perhaps that was just her own experience of Lord Northcott; she had heard that the relationship of father and son could be a difficult one full of any number of pitfalls. Without a brother to study or ask, Clarissa didn't really have the requisite experience to judge. Still, she knew that all was not quite right at Northcott Hall. She had known from the moment she had arrived as a bereaved and afraid young woman of just fifteen years.

The idea of losing the Earl and relying on Philip for the rest of her days did not thrill her. In fact, it made her every bit as afraid as she had been when she'd first arrived. Everything felt so uncertain when she thought of a future without her guardian. And, at eighteen years and soon to be nineteen, she wondered if she would have to suffer with Philip as her guardian until she was one-and-twenty. It did not bear thinking about, for she was certain that he would require her to give over her inheritance as a condition of her continued stay there at Northcott. It wasn't an immense amount, but certainly enough to give her a yearly income for the rest of her life and afford her some rooms in a respectable place if things did not go well at Northcott Hall when Philip became the heir. Of course, that would be if there was anything left of the money if Philip took steps to secure it as soon as his father passed. He did not need the money, of course; it was a speck of dust when compared to what his own fortune would be and it was, of course, held in trust and allotted annually; a well calculated annuity. But Philip was a man who had no charity in his soul whatsoever, always petitioning his father to take breakages out of the servants' meagre wages because *right was right*, as far as he was concerned.

Clarissa sighed, knowing that she was creating a story of the future which did not exist. She vaguely wondered why it was that dreams of the future were always so full of anxiety and fear. If one could dream anything at all, why not let it be a perfect life? But perhaps to prepare for the very worst was just a part of being human.

"You have been very good to me these last years, Clarissa," the Earl said, surprising her, for she had thought him deeply asleep.

"And you have been good to me. Who else would have taken me in?"

"That was a simple enough thing for a man who has so many rooms in his mansion that there are some he has forgotten. My dear, you are not left owing, believe me. It is I who owes you a great debt, for you have listened to my ramblings and stayed with me when I have felt so ill. Perhaps a man should really hope for daughters and not for sons the way that society somehow dictates."

"Thank you, although I am not sure there would be many who would agree," she said and laughed, pleased when she heard him croak a little laughter of his own.

"I used to write everything down in my diaries, Clarissa. Years and years' worth of them in these attics," he said, feebly pointing to the ceiling to indicate the vast array of attics above. "And whilst I still keep a diary by habit, I have turned to it less and less as a friend since you came here. Perhaps *you* have become my friend, Clarissa."

"I would hope so, Lord Northcott. And the friendship has been of great benefit to me too; a girl who had lost her beloved father at fifteen. How quickly you drew me into safety and took his place. I have been very fortunate, and I am very grateful." Clarissa felt a little tearful.

Why was she the one sitting here with a man she was sure did not have long left? Why were his sons not here?

Of course, Felix Ravenswood, the younger of the Earl's two sons, had never lived at Northcott Hall whilst Clarissa had been there. He had left his father's home some time before she'd arrived and she had gathered, over the years, that there was some quarrel between the two of them. Clarissa had seen him so rarely that he was a stranger to her, despite the fact that he did not live far away. She had seen his house from afar, a family home inherited personally from his mother's family, but she had never dared walk too close.

"You have been like a daughter to me, and I have said a prayer of thanks before now that I hope reaches my old friend, Edmund. Still, if my thanks did not reach him, I daresay that I shall be joining him soon enough and will be able to give my message in person, as it were," he said and chuckled weakly.

"Please, you must not say that," Clarissa said, her voice breaking as her eyes filled with tears. "It is too difficult a thing for me to contemplate again."

"Forgive me, my dear," he said, his voice a dry rasp. "I would not wish to hurt you, not for all the world. Goodness knows, I have caused enough pain and heartbreak to others in my life."

"Of course you have not," Clarissa objected.

"You only see me as I am now."

"Why? Were you ever any different?" She dabbed at her eyes with her handkerchief.

"We were all different once. That is what it means to be here; to be human. We make mistakes, we learn, we change. Or at least that is the theory of it all; the purpose of life, perhaps." He sighed and turned his head so that he might look her squarely in the eyes. "But not all of us correct our mistakes, even if we know them to be such. We might learn how we made the mistakes, but I wonder if there can ever be any peace without putting them right."

"What mistakes?" Clarissa was not entirely sure she wanted to know; and yet, at the same time, her attention was rigidly fixed on her guardian.

"Mistakes made so many years ago that even to own up to them now would do no good. That is the thing with mistakes, my dear. We know they are mistakes almost as soon as we have made them, and yet foolish men, men like *me*, try to work with what we have done, to move the world around to fit the new circumstances we have created erroneously. And in doing so, the mistake is no longer a mistake. Instead it becomes a secret. And secrets tear families apart, even if only one person in that family knows what the secret is; that it even *exists*." His voice was trailing away like the last of the birdsong as the night draws down.

Clarissa felt a warm wave of frightened anticipation. Was her guardian about to tell her this secret of his? And would it explain why she had felt the whole household of Northcott Hall to be somewhat off-kilter ever since she arrived? But did she want to know? Did she need to know? She doubted it.

The Earl's eyes were closed again, but he was not at peace. He was muttering under his breath, words she couldn't make out. The perspiration was back, his face now drenched in cold sweat, as was his forehead. Clarissa did what she could to make him comfortable, certain that she should have persisted with the water when she had the chance.

Dr Morton would surely have to be sent for again, although she did not relish the task of finding Philip and telling him so. He behaved in such an exasperated way, as if his father's last weeks, or even days, were nothing but an inconvenience to him. She wondered irresistibly if it had anything at all to do with this secret Lord Northcott had spoken of.

The Earl began to twist and turn in his bed, just as a man suffering a nightmare might do. Clarissa gently shook him by the shoulder, determined to wake him from whatever he was seeing so that he might rest easier once more. His eyes opened for just a moment and he spoke but one word before falling into a deep sleep.
"Felix."

Chapter Two

After leaving the Earl's room, Clarissa decided to ride down into Fowey herself to speak to Dr Morton. For one thing, she did not want to waste time searching Northcott Hall for Philip, and for another, she did not want to have to converse at all with Philip's perpetually dissatisfied wife, Eliza. Neither one of them would be interested and Clarissa would just be left exasperated and upset by the whole experience. Much better to go around them altogether and sort everything out for herself.

So, leaving her favourite maid, Flo Pettigrew, to watch over the sleeping Earl, Clarissa headed to the stables to have her horse saddled.

The day was warm, despite being early Spring, and the ride down into Fowey was pleasant. Her spirits had risen as they always did on such beautiful days, so when she heard the very worst from Dr Morton, those same spirits had so much further to fall, plummeting from a great height.

"Miss Tate, I will certainly call in at Northcott tomorrow and check on the Earl," he began kindly, his gentle Cornish accent so soothing and utterly perfect for a doctor. "But I think I must do you a kindness now, for it strikes me that the care of your guardian falls largely at your feet. Miss Tate, the kindness I shall do you is the truth, and I daresay you won't recognise it as a kindness at all." He paused and looked so sad that Clarissa felt tears filling her eyes, although they did not fall.

"He does not have long, Doctor, I believe that is what you wish to tell me."

"It is days rather than weeks. His body is failing him, and his heart and lungs are so weak that they cannot continue to sustain him. I truly am very sorry, but I have struggled to find a place to rest this information. His son…well," he stopped, clearly not wanting to give voice to his own opinions of the heir to the Northcott Earldom.

"I know. Philip cares very little and I have no easy answer for why that is. Instead, I focus my mind on doing what I can rather than worrying too much about what I cannot change."

"You are wise beyond your years, Miss Tate. Perhaps your own losses in this life have formed your character; strengthened it, I daresay."

"Thank you," she said, recognising and accepting the compliment.

"But his other son," Dr Morton persisted. "There is some rift between them, I believe?" He looked at her a little expectantly.

"I believe so, but I have never known the cause, nor have I ever seen them interact in the years since I arrived at Northcott. Felix Ravenswood inherited Farwynnen House from his grandfather and, I understand, wasted no time in quitting Northcott Hall to take up residence there. He left some time before I arrived in this part of Cornwall. They did not mix in the same circles, for I understand that Felix is somewhat less than a gentleman in his approach to life."

"It is an unusual thing, is it not?" the doctor began. "For I have heard it now and again, but never seen any proof of such a thing. Perhaps it is just something which is easier for people to believe when a man has turned his back on a fine status to live in lesser circumstances. I wonder sometimes, for people do tend to equate a lower standard of living with profligacy, whereas my own work tells me that it is so often the other way around." He had become thoughtful now, as if he had almost forgotten Clarissa was there with him in the austere consulting room of his large riverfront house in Fowey.

"I had never thought of it like that. Felix Ravenswood and I do not have any acquaintances in common," she said, but knew that wasn't entirely true.

Clarissa did now have an acquaintance in common with Lord Northcott's youngest son. However, she had not known Lady Gwendolyn Marchmont for long enough to have discussed the man at all. As far as their conversation regarding Felix Ravenswood had progressed was Lady Marchmont's brief allusion to the fact that he was a regular visitor to her home and a long-standing acquaintance of herself and her husband. Now Clarissa wished that she knew Lady Marchmont well enough to have discovered a little more about the man who ought, by rights, to be living in the fine halls and chambers of Northcott rather than in a wind battered house down on Smugglers' Cove.

"Presumably Felix Ravenswood knows nothing of his father's condition then?" Dr Morton went on.

"No, for I am certain that his brother does not see him at all. I wonder…" she said, and her mind began to whirl.

Perhaps Felix Ravenswood ought to be told of his father's condition. It did not matter what terms they were on; it was in her power to at least give him enough information that he might make up his own mind on the subject. Knowing how disconnected Philip was from his father even as they resided under the same roof, she was certain that it would not occur to him to do what was right in the current circumstances.

But did she really have the courage to make her way down to Farwynnen House and speak to Felix herself? He was a man she had seen but rarely in the years since she had lived at Northcott Hall and they had certainly never been introduced. Perhaps he did not even know of her existence in his father's house. Perhaps he would think that it was not her place to intervene in the affairs of a family she was not a part of.

"I wish I could advise you, Miss Tate, but I daresay it is not my place. All I can do is present you with the facts, and the facts are these; if Felix Ravenswood does not see his father within the next few days, he will never see him again. I fear I have given you a great burden with this news, and much to think about, although I would have you know that it pains me. It really is a matter that Lord Northcott's eldest son should deal with, and yet it seems unlikely that will ever happen. Still, on a more practical note, I will call first thing in the morning if that suits you?"

"That suits me perfectly well, Dr Morton. I really am very grateful to you."

Dr Morton showed her out of his house himself and helped her up onto her horse again with ease. He nodded at her solemnly, a brief and sad smile at its conclusion, as if silently telling her that she could do this; she had the fortitude to manage. Something about his faith in her gave her faith in herself and, as she rode away, she wondered if she really could approach the Earl's youngest son.

Hardly knowing why, Clarissa took a pathway she barely ever took as a rule. It was a pathway she knew would give her a wide berth of Northcott Hall, leading her across the northern end of the Gribben Peninsula and towards the rugged shore on the west. It wasn't a place she ventured into much, despite the fact she liked to walk and ride in the beautiful countryside of that part of Cornwall.

Once she reached the coastal path, she headed south. When she looked back inland, she could make out the vast pitched roof and the dozens of chimneys of Northcott. Sitting square in the centre of the Gribben Peninsular, there was hardly a spot for miles around where that imposing roofline could not be seen. It gave her the strangest sense of being watched, even though she knew it to be impossible. A person would have to sit on top of the great roof of Northcott to be able to see her past the thick shroud of tall trees in the woodland which surrounded the estate on all sides. And who would be watching her anyway? The Earl was too sick and his eldest son too disinterested.

Clarissa knew, of course, that the feeling came from within, and she knew very well why. She had decided, without even a word to herself, to make her way to Farwynnen House and speak to Felix Ravenswood that very day. She was doing so without the authorisation of her guardian, but still she could not turn her horse back. It was as if some invisible golden thread attached to her heart was drawing her inexorably towards Smugglers' Cove. Was it the need to do what was right, or was it something else? For even as she thought about it, Clarissa could sense a little thrill of excitement. Fearful excitement, but it was still excitement, nonetheless.

Felix Ravenswood was an almost indistinct character. She had seen him from afar and that was all. Either from some pews behind her on the rare occasions he attended the Fowey Parish Church, or on the even fewer occasions when she had seen him going about his business in the town. There was one notable occasion when she had been but sixteen or seventeen when she had seen him leaving the home of Sir Hugh Trevithick. Sir Hugh was a man who was better known for turning his drawing room over to card tables for local gentlemen than for his attendance at either the church or the chapel. Nonetheless, he was a well-respected man who had turned a small fortune into a very much larger one with timely investments in the natural resource mining of copper and tin, and there were few who would speak ill of him. He lived in a fine home in Tywardreath, and it had been by chance alone that Clarissa had seen Felix Ravenswood there. She had been with her sister-in-law, Eliza, who had wanted her company to make a visit to a woman she did not like but whose acquaintance she seemed unable to escape. When Eliza saw Felix, she tutted without explanation, a habit Clarissa had since come to understand as being part and parcel of a wholly judgemental character.

Felix had looked back at them and, even across a distance of some fifty yards, Clarissa had been certain she could discern a rather mocking smile. She had certainly heard him chuckle as he swayed this way and that, giving every appearance of being drunk; and in the middle of the afternoon to boot! But Clarissa, as young as she had been, was perhaps not quite so credulous as her older sister-in-law who clearly believed the little performance. For her own part, Clarissa had thought it a little piece of impromptu theatre designed to give Eliza Ravenswood something delicious to take back to her husband; something which Philip might exclaim over for days.

As she neared the dip in the landscape in which she knew Farwynnen House to be contained, Clarissa realised that she did not have Felix Ravenswood's face as part of her memory. Of course, he *must* know of her existence, even as she imagined he did not. They were close enough neighbours, separated only by a distance of a mile and a half of undulating, windswept land. Not to mention the fact that people talked; they passed information this way and that, some of it gossip, most of it of little consequence. Yes, of course, he would know of her existence and the curious place she held within the walls of his childhood home.

Clarissa instinctively slowed her horse to a stop when she saw one of the few chimneys of Farwynnen House hove into view. She was almost on top of the place now, high above the plateau below where that solitary house rested. This was the moment in which she would have to make her decision; should she ride by as she always did, or should she pick her way down the steep path which would lead her to his door?

Chapter Three

In the end, Clarissa made the choice she had known she would make from the start. She jumped down from the saddle and began to lead her horse slowly down that steep path. About halfway down, the beautiful, wild Smugglers' Cove came fully into view in a way it could not from the coastal path above. One had to be *in* Smugglers' Cove to see it properly, and it was a sight which took her breath away.

Clarissa was rooted to the spot for a moment as she stared, open-mouthed, at the small, rugged, sea-battered cove. The rocks were dark, almost black, and as jagged as any along that stretch of coastline. Those rocks curled protective arms around the cove, and she could see the soft and pale sand which formed the smallest beach she had ever seen; that flat, virgin sand surrounded by so much black rock. The further she dropped down into the cove, the more she felt as if she had stepped out of her world and into another. It was so quiet, even more so than the deserted coastal path above. Although she could still feel and hear the wind coming off the sea, the rocky enclosure of the cove afforded a little more protection from it. Still, as she looked out at the sea beyond the cove, just yards away, Clarissa could see how it smashed against the outlying rocks, even on a relatively calm Spring day when its water was a wonderful, inviting shade of blue.

Reaching the bottom of the pathway, Clarissa could now see the entirety of Farwynnen House for the very first time. It was large, although miniscule in comparison to Northcott Hall, with an imposing grey appearance. There were three pitched rooves at different heights, and the stone-mullioned windows were arched, every single one of them. It almost looked like a church, albeit a primitive one. The sort of church that was not pretty like the one in Fowey, but austere; the sort of building one would think twice about before entering. It was thickly built to withstand all that such close proximity to a harsh Cornish sea could throw at it, and Clarissa imagined it to be as cold as the grave on the inside.

And yet, despite all its cold austerity, Clarissa couldn't escape the feeling that it was the most beautiful place she had ever seen. She shook her head, knowing that there wasn't a thing about it to recommend its beauty, and yet there it was. It had an ancient feel, as if it had stood there since the dawn of time, its windows knowing, sightless eyes which bore witness to the rolling sea for day after day; year after year. Perhaps the only witness to decades of smuggling.

The cove had apparently been referred to as Smugglers' Cove for so long that nobody called it Farwynnen Cove any longer. But Clarissa knew that Farwynnen Cove was the name which would be seen on any map of the area. The county-wide enterprise of smuggling had long since dwindled in Cornwall, leaving only a few determined men to carry on the old tradition of avoiding the duties imposed by the government so far away in London. But Farwynnen Cove would undoubtedly be known as Smugglers' Cove for years to come; perhaps even forever.

But all of this was getting her nowhere. It was prevarication and she knew it and, even as she tethered her horse to a solitary post, Clarissa still wondered if she could take the final steps which would bring her to that great wide and arched wooden door, let alone summon the courage to rap at its wind-tortured grain with her gloved knuckles.

"And what are you doing here?" The voice came from behind her, making her gasp with shock.

Clarissa turned sharply to see that Felix Ravenswood must surely have followed her down the steep path from the headland above. But how had he made his way so silently?

"I...I..." she began nervously. "I am Clarissa Tate."

"I know who you are. I did not ask who you were, I asked what you are doing here." He looked vexed and Clarissa realised she was staring up into his face without let-up.

He was a handsome man in a dishevelled sort of way. His hair was wavy and overgrown; a fashionable length, but without the benefit of a slim ribbon at the back of his head holding it all neatly into place, tethering it as so many young men did these days. Instead, it wavered and lifted on the breeze, making him look somehow a part of the nature all around him.

His breeches were well made and well-fitting, although it was clear they had seen better days, as had his heavy black knee boots. His waistcoat was thick and made in a rough woollen fabric, beneath which he wore a clean white shirt. With no tailcoat to smarten his looks, his sleeves were rolled to the elbow as if he had been undertaking some practical, utilitarian work of some kind. But surely an Earl's son would have no need to spend his time in such a way.

The neck of his shirt was wound with a dark cravat, but not worn in the way of a gentleman. Rather it was worn in the style of a fisherman or somebody similar; tied in a knot at the front, the tails hanging down past his collar bone. The shirt itself was a little loose at the neck, displaying his tanned, somewhat weather-beaten skin.

He was dark in every way, with unsettling intense brown eyes, that thick hair, so dark it was almost black, and a heavy, dipped brow. The skin on his face was tanned also and she thought there could not be a man so different from his own brother, for Philip was not a man of the outdoors and his skin always seemed a little sallow.

And yet, for all his apparent roughness, he was a handsome man. A very handsome man. His clothes were well made, even if he wore them in a manner she could only have described as unconventional. All in all, he was both an unsettling and a romantic figure, and Clarissa knew that she would remember this encounter in every detail for the rest of her life.

"Are you simply going to stare at me, Miss Tate, or are you going to answer my question?" He still looked vexed, although she wondered if there was not a little amusement in those dark eyes. He stepped towards her and seized her upper arm. "Well?"

His hand on her arm gave her the most curious sensation. It was such an unusual thing for a gentleman to do, unless the lady in question were unwell in some way and at risk of falling. It was not an aggressive touch, but neither was it gentle. Clarissa made no move to free herself, in part because she was afraid, but largely because she didn't want to. Instead, she decided to answer him at last.

"Forgive me, sir, for intruding upon your privacy, but I have come with a purpose," she began and was pleased to find no evidence in her voice of the little thrum of caution which vibrated gently though her.

"Oh?" he said, staring directly into her eyes and continuing to hold onto her arm.

"I know it is not my place, but nonetheless, I could not keep quiet."

"About what, Miss Tate?" he said, using her name in a way which made her wonder how long he had known it.

"Your father is gravely ill," she said simply, awaiting his response before daring to say any more.

"He is dying?" Felix said and she was certain she saw a look of regret cloud his eyes.

"I fear he is. In truth, Dr Morton tells me that he has days rather than weeks. I have just come from Fowey now, where I spoke to the doctor at length."

"And he has asked for me? My father, I mean," he said, pulling her closer to him when she did not answer. "Well?"

"In a way," she ventured, determined not to let her waning confidence show.

"What do you mean? That does not make sense, Miss Tate." Although he gave the appearance of exasperation, Clarissa could sense immediately that it was every bit the performance that his drunken stumbling had been in Tywardreath just a few years before.

She could see something more, or at least she imagined she did. If she was right, there was a thinly veiled forlornness in his countenance, and it made her sad just to witness it.

"He spoke your name, sir. Just once, and when he was drifting into sleep, but still he said it," she said honestly. *"Felix."* His name on her tongue felt strange, and she had no idea why she had given voice to it so unnecessarily.

Still, he did not seem to have noticed her uncalled-for familiarity, seemingly lost now in his own thoughts.

"And what of my brother? Does he know you are here, Miss Tate?"

"No," she said, unable to find anything better than the truth to respond with.

"Of course not," he said and gave a brief bark of a laugh; a cold and mirthless laugh.

"Sir, it is your business now how you proceed. I can tell you think this none of my concern and goodness knows, you would be right. But I care very much for Lord Northcott and, whilst I do not know you at all, I felt that I ought to at least give you the opportunity to decide for yourself. I truly do not know anything of substance regarding your family or how you came to be so fractured, so I can only act in what I hope is the right way. The rest, sir, is your choice and I shall bid you a good day so that you might make it," she said and gently freed herself from his grip.

"Beyond feelings, I do not know why my family is so fractured either," he said, in a low voice which made it seem as if he spoke to himself. "Still, that does not help now."

Clarissa felt bound to stand there for a moment, even though she had been so determined to walk away. How could he not know what had caused the rift between himself and his own family? Surely that did not make sense.

She was reminded of the Earl's talk of mistakes and how they turned into secrets. Was this somehow connected? Was this important?

Clarissa wanted to be disinterested, but she could not. There was something unspoken at the heart of Northcott, at the heart of the Ravenswood family, and she could feel the unseemly and irresistible desire for that knowledge begin to invade her.

However, she had done all she could do in this current situation, and she was glad she had. Clarissa knew she had been entirely honest in her words; she really had wanted to give father and son one last opportunity in this life; an opportunity to at least say goodbye. Felix Ravenswood's decisions were his to make; his pathway his own to walk. Now was the time for her to go, to walk away and leave this mysteriously isolated man to himself. With a nod, she began to do just that but, when she was but two steps away from him, he caught her arm again and she turned to face him.

"Thank you, Miss Tate. I do not underestimate the courage it took to come here today." His voice was deep and, she thought, a little roughened by emotion; or perhaps it was that way only in her imagination.

Despite the sadness of it all, not to mention the fear, she found the excitement of her choice on that day was undeniable. She had finally met the man, the living myth who was Felix Ravenswood, and she had a curious feeling that nothing in her world would be quite the same again.

"You are welcome, sir," she said gently in reply.

"I will come tomorrow," he said, finally releasing her arm and looking away from her. "Thank you," he said again, walking away from her without a goodbye.

No; nothing was going to be the same again.

Chapter Four

Clarissa sat alone in the vast drawing room of Northcott Hall. Flo Pettigrew had come to her that morning, the very moment Dr Morton had left, and insisted upon her going down for some breakfast and taking a little rest. The rest of the family had eaten, but Cook had seen to it that there was some hearty repast left warm on the serving cabinet in the breakfast room for the young miss, as she always referred to Clarissa.

The Earl's condition had worsened in the early evening and Clarissa had been certain he would expire in the night. Not wanting him to die with no family around him, and not wanting the poor young maid to shoulder the gravest of all responsibilities alone in the darkness, Clarissa had sent Flo to bed and sat with Lord Northcott all night.

He hadn't regained consciousness, but she had talked to him, nonetheless. She talked of the garden, of the begonias and the camellias, of her new acquaintance, Lady Marchmont. Anything but the one thing she was so desperate to tell him; that she had spoken to his youngest son.

She had wanted to tell him she had seen his son look forlorn, that he surely cared about his father. But how could she say any of it when she did not know if Felix Ravenswood would come to Northcott before it was all too late. It would be too cruel to raise her guardian's hopes as he lay slowly dying. It might cause him to hover; a man in physical distress waiting for the son who might never come. She couldn't bare it.

Tears rolled down her face again. Everything seemed to assault her emotions at once. Even the signs that Philip and Eliza had enjoyed a hearty meal that morning had upset her. Their plates were still to be collected and, as Clarissa had helped herself to coffee and nothing more, she wondered how they could find an appetite between them. Philip's father lay dying, Dr Morton had sought him out and made that very clear. How could Philip have then gone on to sit down at the table with his wife, giving no sign that he would make that simple journey upstairs to where his father lay?

Clarissa concentrated on the walls; she didn't want to cry again; it wouldn't help Lord Northcott now. Her tears could wait until there was time to shed them. If Felix Ravenswood did not come, Lord Northcott's departure from this world would have to be handled entirely by Clarissa, with the help of her most trusted maid, Flo. She would have to be strong and giving into her tears whilst the Earl still lived was no way to achieve that aim.

Clarissa blinked, dispelling the tears until the decor of the drawing room came more sharply into focus, no longer blurred and indistinct; no longer distorted by the physical manifestation of her own emotion. She let her mind clear as she stared at the green of the wall coverings; a colour which Eliza had insisted was most fashionable, whilst Clarissa herself thought it too bright and unsettling, with a yellowness to it she didn't like. The ornate surround of the immense fireplace had been painted in the brightest white, so startling a contrast with the walls around it. The detailed plaster scroll work on the ceiling had been similarly painted in white, the silver chandeliers hanging pristine and dust-free from it.

The redeeming feature of the drawing room was, as far as Clarissa could see, the many large windows. They were unobstructed by the matching heavy green curtains which were secured neatly to the side, affording a wonderful view of the grounds to the front of Northcott to anyone of a disposition unable to contemplate such high-fashion decoration for too long.

The pianoforte was set beside the windows, the sunlight reflected a little in the varnished wooden grain. The slight glare transfixed Clarissa for a moment, almost hypnotising her into a sense of much-needed peace. For those few brief moments, she was able to stem the tide of her imminent, inevitable loss. Until she saw a man on horseback in the distance, that was, his journey along the driveway to the house making him appear larger and more distinct with every step.

Clarissa rose from the pale peach brocade covered couch, another affront to a sensitive eye, and made her way with some interest to the window. When the horse and rider were but feet away, she realised who the man was; it was Felix Ravenswood.

Her surprise and relief were so great that her senses were suddenly heightened. The clatter of the horse's hooves seemed impossibly loud on the gravel, as did the approaching footsteps of the hastening stable lad, sent by the stable master to take the gentleman's horse.

As the boy made his approach, there was no sign on his face that he recognised the visitor as the Earl's son. Perhaps the young lad was too young to have any recollection of him, or perhaps he had never seen him before.

When Felix Ravenswood jumped down, Clarissa moved a little to the side, further towards the curtains, in case he should turn and see her looking out of this one of the many, many windows of Northcott Hall.

She studied him in every detail, for he looked a little different from how he had looked upon their first meeting. He wore black breeches with a tailcoat of the same material. His waistcoat was a deep faun colour and his shirt much crisper and more appropriately fitting than the one she had seen him in the day before. He wore a faun coloured cravat tied in the style of a gentleman this time, a stark contrast to his fisherman's style of the previous day. He had gone to some effort, it was clear, and as much as she had secretly liked his rougher appearance of the day before, she was glad that his father, a proud and immaculate man, would not be treated to a similar view of his son.

When she saw Felix look sharply towards the door, she realised that someone must surely have opened it. Felix didn't move towards the steps as any other visitor might, and his countenance was suddenly one of anger. Something was wrong, and Clarissa had to know what.

Hurrying from the room, she crept noiselessly in her soft silk slippers, hardly daring to breathe as she made her way along the wide corridor towards the great entrance hall. She could see Philip in the doorway, his back impossibly straight as if to make himself taller, and she dared to creep a little further along the walls until she was able to hear their conversation.

"Why are you here now? When we have not seen you for so long, why should I admit you?" Philip said, his voice a petulant bark.

"You are not yet the Earl of Northcott, Philip, so you have no status to deny me admittance. I am here to see our father. I know he is ill," Clarissa's heart began to pound; Felix's voice was deeper than Philip's.

It was a man's voice, with a note of uncomplicated confidence to it. It was a far cry from Philip's, that was certain.

"And how do you know that?"

"I have been told, Philip," Felix went on and she heard the sound of his footsteps on the gravel; she knew he was moving closer, even if she could not see him.

"By whom?" Philip snarled and Clarissa felt an uncomfortably cold swathe of perspiration break out across the back of her neck.

"It is common knowledge, Philip. How could it not be when he has been attended so many times by the local doctor? And what difference does it make how I have discovered it? You ought to have told me."

Clarissa breathed a silent sight of relief; he had chosen not to give her away. Still, he likely knew his own brother better than she, and knew how capricious he could be.

"Why? What is it to you? Your relationship to our father is..."

"None of your business," Felix cut him dead.

"It is only a matter of time until I am the new Earl of Northcott, Felix. And since our father is too incapacitated to run things, I naturally speak for him now. You will not be admitted into Northcott, not today nor any other day hereafter. The servants answer to me, and if I tell them to remove you, they shall." There was a self-satisfaction in Philip's voice which made Clarissa despise him.

What a dreadful time to choose to take the upper hand, to use his privilege like a weapon against his own brother, and to have his own father to suffer for it too.

Clarissa began to back away when Philip slowly closed the door. The butler and two footmen had arrived, the confusion at their master opening the door for himself quickly turning into obvious discomfort at the thought of frog-matching the Earl's youngest son from Northcott.

Hurrying back to the drawing room, she closed the door quietly behind her before racing across the room to the window.

She watched in dismay as Felix climbed back up onto his horse, the stable lad who had dashed out to attend him looking every bit as uncomfortable as the servants inside the house had done. Felix looked beaten; a man who realised that he could do nothing about the door being closed on him, both literally and metaphorically.

As he tightened his horse's reins and made ready to turn, he finally looked her way. Clarissa stood frozen behind the glass; her eyes held prisoner by his own, unable to look away. His expression did not change, but he nodded at her, his unspoken thanks for all that she had tried to do for him. When he turned and heeled his horse sharply away, Clarissa felt tears well in her eyes. Had she done the right thing? Or had she simply made an impossible situation so much worse?

Her anger at Philip drove a feeling of utter powerlessness; a feeling that Clarissa Tate had never been fond of. But in that moment, it served its purpose, for in her haste to escape that feeling, something occurred to her. It would be a risk, to her more than to anybody, but it was a risk worth taking, she knew that immediately. This wasn't for her, nor was it even to punish the unconscionable behaviour of Philip. It was for her guardian; it was for the Earl. And it was for Felix, for everybody had a right to say goodbye, whatever had gone before.

And in that very moment, Clarissa knew that she would do it. She could do no other.

Chapter Five

Clarissa bided her time, anxious to be gone but knowing she had to leave a sensible interval to avoid suspicion. She was exhausted from a night without sleep, but made her way up to Flo Pettigrew, who was gently mopping her master's fevered brow when Clarissa walked in.

"Miss Tate! I thought you were to have some rest," Flo whispered, her objection so noble and caring. "I have leave to spend the day with His Lordship direct from Mrs Trelorn; I shan't leave him, Miss."

"I know that, Flo. Really, I do not think I could have managed without you, my dear. But I will only stay a little while. I have an errand to run."

"Can it not wait? You look so tired, Miss. I do reckon if you were to ask Mrs Trelorn, she would send someone else out to run your errand for you."

"Flo, you are so kind, but my errand is something I must do for myself. In truth, it is something I must keep secret."

"If anyone should ask for you, what should I say?"

"In the most unlikely event that anybody comes to enquire, you may tell them that I have gone to Fowey again to speak to Dr Morton. It will do as well as any other lie," she said, regretting that she must involve Flo in all of this, but knowing her so well that she could trust her to be absolutely discreet.

"I shall do just that, Miss. Be sure to tell the same to the stable-lad if he's so cheeky as to ask, for he has a want of asking too many questions," Flo said, knowing the workings of Northcott Hall better than anyone.

"Bless you, Flo," Clarissa rested her hand on Flo Pettigrew's shoulder before taking her leave.

By the time she had made her way outside, thankfully not encountering either Philip or Eliza along the way, Clarissa was eager to be gone. The stable lad, still a little unsteady after the embarrassment of earlier, did not indulge his rumoured tendency toward inquisitiveness, saddling her horse and helping her up into the saddle without comment.

Clarissa idled along on her horse, fighting an urge to set off at a canter immediately. As keen as she was to find Felix, she couldn't risk a casual observer wondering at her haste. With her plan already fraught with danger, exciting suspicion of any kind was out of the question. When she reached the turn in the long gravel drive and knew she would finally be out of sight, she urged her horse on, the sudden change in speed pulling her bonnet back a little along her thick brown hair.

By the time she reached the undulating, wind swept ground of the Gribben Peninsula, she was moving at a pace she was far from used to. But far from frightening herself, Clarissa felt a strange and uncommon sense of exhilaration. She felt so sure that she was doing the right thing that she felt none of the nervousness she had felt on her first visit to Farwynnen House.

As soon as she was within sight of its roof, its few chimney tops, Clarissa slowed her pace and looked behind her. The peninsula was deserted all around her, and so she halted her horse and slid down from the saddle, leading him onto the steep path down to Farwynnen House without delay.

There was not time to silently acknowledge the wild beauty of the cove this time, she simply hoped and prayed that he would be there. If he had ridden away elsewhere, her plan would come to naught.

Hearing the unmistakable whinnying of a horse, Clarissa tethered her own and followed the sound. It led her around the front of Farwynnen house, where she turned and walked slowly along the side. There stood a small stable block, where the son of the Earl of Northcott was removing the saddle from his own horse, no sign of the ever-ready help that was always on hand to the occupants of Northcott Hall.

She cleared her throat loudly to announce her arrival, and he turned sharply to look at her.

"Miss Tate?" he said, his surprise clear.

"Forgive my intrusion into your affairs once more, but I must speak to you," she began, wishing now that she had ordered her thoughts and practiced her conversation en route.

"Is it my father?" he said, looking as if he feared the worst.

"There is no change in Lord Northcott's condition, sir. Forgive me for having you think so. No, I am here because I heard all that passed between you and your brother at the hall. I want to apologise."

"It was not your doing. You have nothing to apologise for," he said and sighed with a hint of exasperation before turning his attention back to his horse.

"Come to the hall tonight and I will take you to see you father," she was keen to get to the crux of her plan. "I will be waiting for you in the morning room. Come to the glass doors and I will let you in."

"What are you talking about?" he said and looked at her incredulously.

"But please make it as late as possible. Perhaps you could come at three o'clock in the morning, when I can be sure that the household are sleeping. That will give you until almost five o'clock, when the servants begin to rise. I shall be sitting with your father tonight, so nobody will be there to stop you seeing him."

"I must crawl into Northcott like a thief in the night, must I?" he said, although he looked more resigned than angry.

"I can do nothing about the outer circumstances of all this. I have no place of importance at Northcott, for I am only Lord Northcott's ward," she said, hoping he would not let go of the opportunity for the sake of pride and nothing better.

"Forgive me, now is not the time to let my anger take control of me," he said and swept a hand down over his face; he looked as exhausted as Clarissa, and she wondered if he, too, had suffered a night without sleep.

"There is no apology necessary. I saw and heard your brother's behaviour and I felt angry too. He should not have said what he said, and he most certainly ought not to have refused you your father's bedside."

"You do not like my brother, Miss Tate?"

"My presence here and now must surely answer your question. If Philip discovers my intentions, I will likely be denied a home and my own opportunity to say goodbye to the man who took me in when my beloved father died. So no, I do not like your brother," she laughed mirthlessly. "What more trouble could I be in than this, if I am discovered? What harm in stating my feelings honestly?"

"You are a most unusual young woman," he said, his face almost expressionless so that she did not know if it was a compliment or an insult.

"I daresay."

He was quiet for some moments as he finally removed his horse's saddle and walked into the little stable, setting it high on the stone wall of one of the stalls. Clarissa took a couple of steps forward whilst his back was turned, not at all sure why she did such a thing.

"I will come to the morning room door, Miss Tate," he said without warning, his back still to her as he took a brush down from a wooden shelf. "At the appointed hour, of course," when he turned, he was smiling at her.

"Very well," she said and nodded, her relief at his acceptance almost dizzying.

She wanted him to come; she wanted him to see his father one last time. She just didn't know why she was so invested in it all. Clarissa was so fond of the Earl and knew she would be terribly saddened by his passing when it came, but surely his relations with his son, a thing he had never discussed with her at all, were none of her concern.

"In spite of every appearance, I really am very grateful to you. And despite the obvious distance between my father and myself, I cannot turn my back on this final opportunity for us to make some sort of peace," he surprised her with his candour, for most men of such status were rigid and tight-lipped.

It was on the tip of her tongue to say that he was a most unusual person too, but she caught herself just in time.

"I suppose you know the grounds well enough to approach without being seen?" she said, keen to impress upon him the importance of not being caught.

"I did not give you away earlier, and I shall not give you away tonight," his dark eyes were intense, pinning hers with an almost physical force.

"I know, and I am grateful to you for it," she said, wanting to turn her head, to look away and escape that gaze, but unable to do so.

"You take a great risk in all of this and I do not underestimate the courage it takes you to do so."

This was the second time in as many days that this man, all but a stranger to Clarissa, had praised her courage and in almost exactly the same way. It had a tremendous effect on her, and she knew she would not willingly let this man down. There was something about him; something which made her long to know a little more of him.

She wanted to hear the truth of things, not the bile which Philip and Eliza spouted so freely; the tales of inebriation and low standards. For how could she trust a word to come from Philip's mouth? A man who would deny his own father such a fundamental right without so much as a consultation. What sort of man was Felix Ravenswood really, when the rumour and self-serving narration were peeled away and discarded? The Earl had never spoken of him to her, nor had he heard his eldest son disparage Felix in his presence. Did he feel the same way? Did he believe the same things? Or was there something the Earl could tell her that would shed light on the character of this mysterious, mesmerising man? How she wished Lord Northcott had at least told her something.

"I must return now to Northcott, for I do not want to prompt suspicion if my absence is noted," she said, wanting to stay but knowing there was no real cause now for her to linger.

She had offered her plan, and she had told him every part of it. They were still strangers, and there were no loose ends for them to tie.

"Of course," he said, setting down his horse's brush and walking back along the side of the house with her.

He untethered her horse without a word and, in that same silence, he lifted her up onto the saddle with ease, surprising her a little.

"Until tonight, Miss Tate," he said.

"Until tonight," she parroted his words.

Her horse made a minor objection to carrying her up the steep slope but managed it with ease in the end. As soon as Clarissa reached the coastal path above, she looked back, but her view of the cove and the house was, as always, obscured. She had no idea if he still stood there or not but hoped that he did. Why it mattered was a mystery to her; perhaps it was nothing more than the strange unreality of the day and a night without sleep.

It was time to go back to the hall now, to take up her seat beside her guardian and hope to have a little rest before the long night ahead. The only thing keeping her going was the idea that she had begun to right the wrong she had seen Philip do; it gave her a little thread of energy upon which she hoped she could rely for many hours to come.

Chapter Six

By the time night came, Clarissa was mercifully a little rested. Flo Pettigrew had kept silent vigil over the Earl, asking no questions at all as Clarissa slept soundly in the chair by the window. When she awoke just two hours later, Clarissa felt surprisingly rested, if a little stiff from sleeping in the chair.

As her eyes began to focus, Clarissa could see Flo gently dabbing at the Earl's brow with a damp cloth.

"Has he woken at all?" Clarissa said gently.

"No, Miss. He has stirred once or twice, but he has not opened his eyes," Flo said sadly.

"I wonder if he will ever come around again before he…" She closed her eyes against tears which threatened.

"I hope so, Miss. I am sure he would like to say goodbye to you after all your kindness," Flo had risen to her feet and tentatively patted Clarissa's shoulder.

"Has the Earl's son or daughter-in-law been in to see him at all?" Clarissa didn't want to embarrass the young maid, but she wanted to know.

"No, Miss," Flo said quietly, her eyes turned down to the Oriental rug on the floor. "I reckon it's a terrible shame, isn't it?"

"It is, Flo. It is quite unforgivable," Clarissa's voice was a near whisper, although she didn't expect for a moment that either Philip or Eliza were about to stride into the room.

"If only one of his sons would be here at the end, Miss. I know I shouldn't speak of it, it isn't my business, but His Lordship was always very kind to me," Flo's eyes filled with tears, surprising Clarissa who took the maid into her arms for a moment to comfort her.

"We will do our very best for him, Flo. Even if he does not wake, he will know that two people who care for him very much are here watching over him." She released her, giving her a fresh handkerchief from her own sleeve.

"He will, Miss. Thank you," Flo said and dried her eyes.

In that moment, Clarissa almost confided in Flo Pettigrew. She was such a kind young woman, one whom Clarissa knew would most certainly keep her secret. But she knew also that it was unfair to expect a maid in that household to know such a secret in the first place. If it ever came to light that she had been aware of Clarissa's determination to sneak Felix Ravenswood into Northcott Hall, Philip would undoubtedly dismiss her without a reference and without a care for how the young woman who had served their house so well and for so long would survive.

The two women spent the rest of the day in the Earl's chamber, having their meals sent to them and not venturing into any other part of the hall. The Earl had not regained consciousness and had barely stirred for some hours, causing Clarissa to worry that he would never know that Felix had come to see him. Perhaps all she could do was pray that he lived long enough for that final meeting to take place, if only for Felix's sake.

As night began to draw down, Clarissa declared that she would, for a second night, nurse the Earl alone. Flo had worked hard all day and Clarissa had taken a little rest, so she would brook no argument and the maid eventually acquiesced, leaving her at ten o'clock.

Clarissa spent the next few hours trying to concentrate upon the book she had open on her lap, but in all that time did not read enough to warrant even turning a page. Her nerves were beginning to interfere with her concentration, assaulting her with images of all the ways in which her plan could go wrong.

She imagined Felix being apprehended in the grounds by a particularly vigilant footman, or worse still, being found in the Earl's chamber by Philip himself. Of course, that would require him to have an attack of conscience in the middle of the night. If he could not find conscience by day, she very much doubted he would find it in his sleep. Nonetheless, to play out the worst-case scenario in her mind was curiously irresistible.

At half past two, Clarissa decided to make her way down to the morning room. She would go by the light of a single candle in a holder and, should she encounter anybody at all, she would claim to be making her way to the kitchen to help herself to a little bread-and-butter. It was to be a long night for her, with or without Felix Ravenswood, and nobody would suspect anything amiss in her story.

However, as she tiptoed silently through the house, her slippers making no sound on the stairs or through the hall below, she began to feel a little more confident. She hovered at the bottom of the stairs, listening intently and hearing nothing but the ticking of the enormous grandfather clock. It really was the middle of the night, and the house was truly asleep.

She crept into the morning room, closing the door behind her and hastening across to the large glazed doors. She peered out into the night, but even the gloom of the solitary candle was enough to render her vision of the outside world blind.

With almost half an hour to wait, Clarissa set the candle down on a side table, taking a seat in the chair closest to the glazed doors. She closed her eyes so that she might listen intently, remaining vigilant to any noise which would suggest movement within the house. And despite her somewhat heightened nervous state, her closed eyes and her concentration began to feel very comfortable indeed. She could feel herself sliding into sleep and knew that she mustn't, in spite of her mind trying to tell her that only a few minutes couldn't hurt. She was in just that state of near slumber when the faintest tap on the glass doors made her sit up straight, her eyes wide and her heart pounding.

Clarissa rose to her feet and hurried to the door, opening it slowly, hoping that there would be no tell-tale squeak or creek. There was nothing, and Felix stepped noiselessly inside.

"Thank you," he leaned forward and whispered into her ear.

She nodded in response, and then lifted the candle from the side table and began to make her way from the room. They both stopped at the door and she opened it just a little, peering out into the corridor beyond. She could see nothing and hear nothing and, in the end, knew that they must start moving.

They reached the Earl's chamber with surprising speed and she was pleased that Felix, true to his word, had done everything in his power not to give her away. Once they were inside with the door closed behind them, she relaxed. She turned the key in the lock, having already decided that, should she hear anybody approaching, she would have to force Felix to hide under his father's bed. But of course, she was confident now that nobody would come. It was the journey through the house which had been the only true danger point, and she knew it. And, since that dangerous journey did not have to be made again for an hour or so, Clarissa decided to put it from her mind; there were more important things at hand.

Felix walked slowly into the room, almost cautiously, as if there was some danger. But Clarissa quickly realised that he was afraid of what he might see, afraid of how his father might look in his final illness.

"He looks so peaceful," Felix said, turning to her, looking into her eyes, before closing the gap and sitting down on the chair she had left at the side of the Earl's bed. "And he does not look so ill, does he? I mean, I know that he is a man at the very end of his life, but he still looks broad-shouldered and vital as he lays there. I am glad that he looks strong, even now," he finished and Clarissa, unsure of what she ought to do, crossed the room to the chair beneath the window, the one she had slept in earlier in the day.

"I do not expect you to sit out of things, Miss Tate. You are the only person in this house who truly cares for my father and you have every right to be at his bedside. Here, I will bring that chair across the room for you," he said and strode to her, lifting the large rattan chair with ease and setting it down on the other side of his father's bed.

Clarissa sat down, feeling a little awkward to be such a close witness to the final meeting between father and son. She felt like an interloper, but the feeling quickly left her when Felix began to speak to his father.

"Father I am here, it is Felix. I wish I knew what to say to you. Perhaps I shall just tell you something I am sure you already know." Although he was speaking quietly, his voice was deep and easily discerned. "I never understood why things were as they were between you and my mother, and I wish I could have found some way to forgive it, but I cannot. I loved her, you see, as I love you, and so I was in a most dreadful position. But I have not come here to go over the old ground, the things which we could never straighten out between us in life. I am here to tell you that I love you, Father, that I have missed you and always will. But I have a good life, one in which I am content, and so you may rest easy without any concerns for me."

Clarissa was transfixed, unable to take her eyes off Felix Ravenswood. In the pale-yellow light of the Earl's chamber, Felix looked darker than ever. His dark brown hair looked almost black, his eyes blacker, and his heavy brows dipped sorrowfully.

Her attention was drawn away only when the Earl himself began to stir, his arms and hands moving as he sought to free himself from the warm blankets that Clarissa and Flo Pettigrew had tightly tucked around him. As soon as his hands were free, he reached out towards Felix, blindly following the sound of his son's voice. If nothing else, surely, he had heard what Felix had said. Clarissa could only hope that he had, that he would know that his son had come and that he loved him.

"Felix, my dear boy," the Earl began, his throat dry and his voice a thin rasp. "You came home at last. You are in your rightful place."

His eyes began to flicker open, so pale and watery as they fought for the focus needed to see Felix come into view. He blinked and blinked, a slow smile finally spreading across his face, a clear indication that he could see his youngest son most clearly.

Reminded of the passing of her own father, Clarissa found herself assaulted by emotions of the very saddest kind. It was made all the sadder by the idea of the years wasted, time in which these two men could have enjoyed each other's company, even the often-unspoken love between a father and son.

"I am here, father," Felix said and finally took the Earl's hand between both of his own.

"Do not be unkind to Philip, it is not his fault," the Earl said, his eyes already beginning to close.

"No, of course," Felix said, and Clarissa was certain that he didn't understand his father's words, but knew that there was not time for such discussion.

"Good night, my boy. My Felix," the Earl said as his body seemed suddenly to go limp.

"Good night, Father," Felix said, and he stared as his father's head as it lolled on the pillow, the life finally all gone.

Clarissa knew then that the Earl had waited for his son. Even in unconsciousness, he had clung to life so that he might have this last moment. He had known, somehow, that Felix would be there, and the wonder and sadness of it all was suddenly too much. Tears were rolling down her face, and she searched in her sleeve for the handkerchief she had given away to Flo Pettigrew earlier. Instead, she was forced to brush her tears away with her hand.

Felix finally let his own head fall, and she saw him sweep a hand across his eyes, knowing that he had shed some tears of his own. Nothing was ever going to be the same again, she knew that, just as she had known it in the moment that her own beloved father had died. And, just as was the case with her father, she knew she would miss the old Earl so very much.

Unable to help herself, Clarissa began to cry in earnest. Felix rose to his feet, rubbing at his face with both hands until all traces of his own tears were gone. He walked around the bed to where she sat in the rattan chair and she could feel his presence behind her. He laid a hand on the top of her head, still at first, and then gently stroking her thick brown hair.

Felix took a handkerchief from his pocket and pressed it into her hand, saying nothing as he continued to gently stroke her hair.

"Thank you," she said when she had gained control of herself once more.

"I think the gratitude is, quite rightly, all mine. Thank *you*, Miss Tate," he said, and she felt his hand slide away.

She rose to her feet, she knew she must, and stood before him, clearly able to see the grief in those eyes which looked so black. What on earth had happened to keep them apart? What was the secret the Earl had spoken of just days before? And what would it matter if she discovered it now, surely it was all too late?

"I will never forget what you have given me this night, Miss Tate. Please know that you may rely upon me from this moment onward in any situation at all. You may ask for my help at any time and know that I shall give it." He was staring at her intently and she had no idea how to respond.

"I do not like to ask you to leave, sir, but I think I must take you back through the house now. I am glad he saw you, for your father had been unconscious for so long, I did not expect him to awaken before the end. I do believe he was waiting for you," she said, starting to feel emotional again.

"I am glad he waited. I am glad you were here to interpret his silent wishes. But I will never speak of this to anybody, I will not have you suffer for your moral courage. My brother will never hear of this; nobody shall. And as for showing me back through the house, I shall find my own way in the dark without incident. Take great care of yourself, Miss Tate." And with that, he reached for her hand and drew it towards him, kissing the back of it before releasing her.

Without another word, he turned and silently made his way out of the room.

Chapter Seven

It had been a real treat to receive an invitation card from Lady Gwendolyn Marchmont and Clarissa had experienced a feeling of freshness and hope. She had hardly been out of the house, and not off the estate at all, in the three months since the Earl had died.

In her own way, Clarissa was observing a period of mourning, even though she was no blood relation of the old Earl. She had noted more than once that it was more respect than either Philip or Eliza had cared to pay. Eliza might well be wearing staid colours, but she had not kept to the house as Clarissa had. Philip had arrogantly declared that, as the new Earl, he had a great many responsibilities, and social activities with people of the county was just one of them. And what fine Earl could do so without his fine Countess by his side? Clarissa thought them both anything but fine.

"Lord Northcott, I have been invited this afternoon to take tea with Lady Marchmont," Clarissa said shyly over breakfast. "I wonder if I might go," she added, hating to seem to ask his permission.

The greatest kindness of her old guardian's will had been the mention of the fact that he had signed away Clarissa's guardianship in the weeks before his death, claiming her to be of sound morals and sensible ways, so much so that her early emancipation was one of his last acts performed on this earth. Of course, no conversation had ensued, and Clarissa still did not know what this would mean in practice now. Philip seemed hardly to have taken in the announcement, likely because he could not have cared any less about the matter. For Eliza's part, she seemed to be so pleased that Clarissa must now address her as *Lady Northcott* that no mention had been made of Clarissa's own circumstances. At least, for the time being, Philip had not demanded Clarissa turn over her yearly allowance to him. In that respect, perhaps any conversation pertaining to her future ought not to be attempted. Hers were unusual circumstances and likely open to the interpretation of the current Earl.

"Yes, go," Philip said, barely looking up from his plate of kidneys and hot tomatoes.

"I do not like Lady Marchmont very much. She is a little too forthright and opinionated for my taste," Eliza said waspishly as Clarissa stifled a sudden urge to laugh; she had never met anybody more opinionated than Eliza.

Clarissa stayed silent. She wanted to defend her newest friend but thought better of it. Eliza was as capricious as her husband, and to offer a different viewpoint might mean that she would not be allowed such wonderful company that afternoon as she had hoped. She smiled sweetly, the only means by which she could remain politic.

Clarissa enjoyed the ride over to the Marchmont's large townhouse in St Austell. Their main residence was Marchmont Hall in Truro, but being a new acquaintance, Clarissa had not yet been there. It was common knowledge that Lord and Lady Marchmont spent a good deal of time in St Austell, more time than in Truro. Lady Marchmont preferred it, being closer to the landscape of her childhood and enjoying the slightly less rigid society to be had there.

"My dear Miss Tate, how relieved I am to see you," Lady Marchmont, alone in the drawing room, hastened across the large Persian rug to great Clarissa with enthusiasm. "I have not set eyes on you since the Earl's funeral. I had begun to think you had expired yourself. You have been so elusive, like the morning dew evaporating in the warm sunshine."

"I have kept to Northcott in mourning. Well, my own little version of it, for I know I was never a relation." Clarissa felt a little silly giving her explanation.

"Oh, how kind you are. I think I like how you make your own little customs. To do so is a fine indication of courage, in my opinion," she went on, surprising Clarissa, who glowed a little under the praise of the older woman.

Gwendolyn Marchmont was a well-known figure in Cornwall society, but she was not to everybody's taste. Eliza had been right to say she was forthright, for she was, but in what Clarissa had come to think of as a rather refreshing way. She was clever and did nothing to hide it, which was probably the biggest reason for a little silent scorn from some of her more traditional female acquaintances, and she was a very tall woman who stood up straight; she would no more hide her towering height than her intellect. For Clarissa, she was an irresistible figure, one she was proud to have managed to gain the respect of.

"Thank you, Lady Marchmont," Clarissa smiled a little shyly.

"Come in and sit down, my dear. The tea will be here any moment and we have so much to talk about. I have missed you, really I have. Mrs Nancarrow's bridge game has not been the same without you," she went on, and ushered Clarissa into a seat on the bright red brocade-covered couch.

The town house was very modern and Lady Marchmont's taste, like her demeanour, was far from muted. Clarissa liked it very much but thought that there wasn't another person in all of Cornwall who could have made it work so well.

"Thank you. I really am glad to have come here today. I have felt so low and I doubt wandering the halls and corridors of Northcott have done much to improve things."

"No indeed," Lady Marchmont said and winced. "But I knew you would be greatly affected by Lord Northcott's passing. My dear, you looked so sad at the funeral and I wished I could have spirited you away. I could have brought you here."

"Oh, that is kind of you."

"It was well-attended. The funeral, I mean."

"Yes, it was. I knew he was a popular man, but I had never realised how popular. At such events, so many people turn out simply to satisfy curiosity or to say that they were at an Earl's funeral. Even more would seek to curry favour with the new Earl, and I am bound to say I saw my fair share of that," Clarissa said, pleased that she had Lady Marchmont's rapt attention. "But for the most part, neither was the case. People genuinely came to pay their respects."

"I was glad that Felix Ravenswood chose to attend. In fact, I never doubted it, not for a minute," Lady Marchmont said.

"No, I did not doubt it either," Clarissa said, not wanting to wander too far down a dangerous path.

It had certainly come as no surprise to Clarissa when she saw Felix Ravenswood at his father's graveside. He did not hover near the back, keeping out of the way, but rather he had made his way to the very front of things, exchanging no words with anybody as he silently bid a final farewell to his father.

Clarissa had seen how irritated Philip was by his brother's attendance, and it made her angry. Felix Ravenswood had been forced to sneak into the house in the dead of night to make that final peace with his father. Philip had been residing under the same roof and had still had the temerity to be annoyed to have been woken in the early hours to be told of his father's passing when, in his opinion, such news could have waited until the morning. How dare Philip be made irritated by anything?

Clarissa had tried not to stare at Felix throughout the service, but her eyes were drawn to him time and time again. He was a capable man, a seemingly self-sufficient man, but surely everybody needed a little support at the funeral of a family member. Perhaps they needed that support all the more when the relationship between themselves and the deceased had been an awkward one. She had wanted to reach out, to move to stand closer to him, to let him know that he wasn't alone. But, of course, any such public move of that nature would have been punished by Philip, she was sure of it. In the end, their eyes had met and Felix, still careful not to give her away, gave the barest nod, so slight that nobody else present would have recognised it as such.

"I wish I knew what had come between them, Lady Marchmont. Not out of curiosity, but out of sadness. There is no doubt in my mind that father and son loved one another but there was something there in the way, some great barrier to their relationship." If she was honest, Clarissa was wondering if Lady Marchmont had any better idea than she did.

"Well, I doubt we'll ever know. Felix most certainly won't talk about it, and I have tried. Well, you know I am a little forward, I suspect," she gave a mischievous sort of grin that made Clarissa like her more and more.

"It is a shame, for I have no doubt that it hurt them both."

"I have known Felix Ravenswood for a long time and have always been able to see that there is a tear in his heart; a great long jagged tear. I cannot imagine that it will ever be mended, but I can hope for it. If only they had been reconciled before the Earl died. I do have a romantic heart, you see, underneath all this, and I firmly believed that a reconciliation at the end would have constituted the pathway to recovery for Felix. Despite the rumours about him, I like Felix Ravenswood very much and my husband is a great friend of his also."

"Well, perhaps in the end they…" Clarissa said, trying to give Lady Marchmont hope of a happier future for her friend but realising she had embarked upon it in a way that would undoubtedly give her away to such a clever, shrewd woman.

"They *were* reconciled," Lady Marchmont said, and it was not a question. "I cannot tell you the peace that gives my own heart."

"Lady Marchmont, I have perhaps spoken a little too freely. You see, Philip, Lord Northcott I should say, does not know. If he were to find out, I would be…"

"You helped Felix, did you not? You did, I can see it in your eyes!"

"Lady Marchmont, please," Clarissa could hear her own tone of pleading.

"I will never give you away, Miss Tate. Goodness, I cannot imagine how you achieved such a thing and I shall not ask you for any of the details. I am just glad that there was, in the end, somebody of sense and good heart on Felix's side." When Lady Marchmont had finished speaking, Clarissa was surprised to see her take a handkerchief from the sleeve of her gown and dab at her eyes; she doubted that this woman was one who was easily moved to tears and so her sudden upset, albeit well contained, had a great effect on Clarissa.

"Forgive me, I did not mean to upset you," Clarissa said.

"I am not upset, my dear, I am touched. I knew there was a good reason I was so drawn to you at Mrs Nancarrow's bridge game week after week. There you are! I am praising myself as a good judge of character." She laughed. "Well, I know I am," Lady Marchmont brightened considerably and Clarissa realised that it had taken her some effort to recover.

"I will take that as a compliment," Clarissa smiled broadly. "Oh, and tea is here," she added when a maid slid silently into the room with a tray.

"Oh, how lovely!" Lady Marchmont had gathered herself entirely. "And bread-and-butter too. Oh, how I adore bread-and-butter. Thank you, Violet," she finished, and the maid smiled, curtsied, and disappeared from the room.

"You have been a good friend Felix, Miss Tate," Lady Marchmont began again as she poured their tea.

"I hardly know him, Lady Marchmont. He never lived at Northcott Hall whilst I have been there, and he has not been a visitor. I have only ever seen him from afar, and only have Philip's opinion of him. *Lord Northcott's* opinion of him," she said, correcting herself. "Which is never very good and, I am starting to realise, perhaps a little overdone."

"Oh yes, the drunkenness, gambling, and womanising, I suppose?" Lady Marchmont said with a loud and scandalised laugh. "Oh, how delicious!"

"Yes, I suppose that is the crux of it," Clarissa said lightly, hoping to hide the fact that her interest was now piqued.

"I do believe that Philip Ravenswood is what might be described as a one trick pony," Lady Marchmont was highly amused.

Even sitting down, Lady Marchmont's great height was easy to discern. Clarissa liked the way that she still sat up ramrod straight, her long neck extended, her head full of barely contained thick dark hair pinned back. She wore a silk headband around her head, resting around the crown. It matched her peach gown, which was just a little flamboyant for an afternoon tea but again, something which Lady Marchmont wore very well. The headband was modern and youthful, a little note of high fashion that Clarissa liked. She was not terribly fashionable herself, and she certainly didn't have any expectations of how others should look, but there was something about Lady Gwendolyn Marchmont that made it all fit, as if it somehow described her. A woman who, in her late forties, must surely have a great experience of life and yet, at the same time, a youthful spirit and a determination not to fit any particular mould. How could she not be intrigued by a woman like that? How easy it was to like her.

"You do not think the things which Felix Ravenswood's own brother says about him are true?" Clarissa said, wheedling for a little information.

It had been three months since she had last set eyes on him; three months since the funeral of the old Earl. Clarissa had to admit to herself that he did cross her mind regularly. He crossed her mind every day.

"Well, perhaps I will not say. Perhaps I ought to let you decide for yourself. You are an intelligent woman and one who is not in the common way. You are not a part of the *herd* in society, I could tell that about you immediately." She paused thoughtfully, her eyebrows dipping before she came to some silent decision, smiled, and nodded furiously. "Yes, I think it would be rather fun to have you work Felix Ravenswood out for yourself. I have a feeling that you will find out even more about him than I ever have. Do not ask me how I know that, I just do. I have a firm feeling about this." She was smiling mischievously. "Yes, that is settled."

"What is settled?"

"Do not look so worried," Lady Marchmont started to laugh. "Now, let us set about this bread-and-butter before it goes dry and curly," she finished, clearly stalling in a way which made Clarissa suspect that she was never going to get an answer to her question; not in words, at any rate.

Chapter Eight

If she was entirely honest, Clarissa had not looked forward to the ball at the home of Lord and Lady Sedgwick at all. It was the first time since the old Earl had passed that Philip and Eliza had shown any sort of interest in her, and that interest made her a little wary.

Eliza had been particularly attentive, making her own lady's maid available to Clarissa and declaring that she really was a true wonder when it came to hair. In the three years Clarissa had lived at Northcott Hall, Eliza had never once taken a single moment's interest in anything about her, much less her appearance.

Clarissa tried to take it all on face value, telling herself that Eliza's maid really had done wonders with her hair, taming her thick dark waves into a smooth and fashionable pleat on the back of her head before painstakingly forming beautiful shining ringlets at the front by tying thick strands of hair up in rags. The whole process had taken the better part of the day and Clarissa, perhaps not as involved in that side of life as she ought to be, felt a little exhausted by it. The end result, however, was very pleasing and Clarissa spent a little longer than usual admiring her appearance in the long oval gilt-framed mirror in her chamber.

Eliza had made a great fuss over her gown too, choosing a colour from Clarissa's wardrobe herself which she declared suited her skin tone very well indeed. It was a light but strangely vibrant blue, like cornflowers which had faded at the end of the Summer, and Clarissa had to admit that Eliza had made a good choice for her. It had short sleeves and the colour was set off to even better advantage by the addition of brand-new long white gloves which Eliza had given her.

Of course, Clarissa was every bit as clever as Lady Marchmont had declared, and she knew that nothing came without a price, not even a pair of gloves. From that moment onward, she was absolutely on her guard, listening keenly to every scrap of conversation which passed between husband and wife, and keeping her eyes peeled at the ball for anything that seemed a little out of the ordinary.

In the end, Clarissa need not have bothered. The effort she had put into such keen observations had not been required, for Philip and Eliza's aim in taking her to the ball with them and being so uncharacteristically attentive very quickly became apparent. And it became apparent in the form of a young man called Daniel Morgan.

The ball was well attended, not to mention quite clearly enjoyed, with people keenly taking part in the dancing, chattering with their neighbours, and exclaiming over the plentiful buffet tables. Lord and Lady Sedgwick were extremely attentive, but Clarissa imagined that was the newfound status of their guest rather than any true warm feelings towards the new Earl and Countess of Northcott. It sickened her a little, but not so much that she tuned against Lord and Lady Sedgwick; she had always liked them well enough.

Despite all the movement and conversation, Clarissa could sense she was being watched. She looked back at the young man who was staring at her, so carefully that he would never have known that she had realised his determined study of her. He was tall and slim, his back ramrod straight, and his hair such a bright blonde that it drew the eye. A handsome young man of perhaps middle to late twenties, Clarissa was sure that more than one young lady would be pleased with such attention. In her case, however, his close scrutiny was unwanted and made her feel somehow cornered. Not just cornered by his attention but cornered by a wider scheme she knew nothing about. Whilst she might know nothing about it, she was already forming her suspicions.

After a while, Philip drifted away, and it was no surprise to Clarissa that he walked straight from her to the staring young man. She watched him leave, staring at his back as he walked away.

"That gown really does suit you, my dear," Eliza said, overdoing her praise in a way which immediately told Clarissa she was distracting her.

"Thank you. Your gown also suits you very well," Clarissa said hurriedly, not taking her eyes from the little meeting happening just feet away.

"Are you enjoying the ball, Clarissa?" Eliza went on.

"Yes, very much," Clarissa said and could hear the distraction in her own voice; something was happening, something she was not privy to, and it made her feel that the control of her life was somehow slipping through her fingers.

In that moment, she inexplicably remembered Felix's words on the night they had borne witness to the last moments of the old Earl, *"Please know that you may rely upon me from this moment on in any situation at all."* His voice in her head made the back of her neck tingle and she then, in turn, shivered.

"Are you quite all right?" Eliza said, eyeing her curiously.

"Yes, thank you," Clarissa said, feeling a horrible swirling sensation in her stomach as she watched Philip and the young blond man approach. "Who is that?" she said a little abruptly as she turned to Eliza.

"Oh, that is Daniel Morgan, I believe," Eliza said, clearly taken off guard by the sudden question. "A very nice young man, by all accounts," she added with a little more firmness and conviction.

There wasn't time for Clarissa to ask anything else, for the little party of two had suddenly arrived. Before he had even spoken, there was already something about Daniel Morgan that Clarissa could not warm to. Perhaps it had been his determined staring, or perhaps it was the idea that they all knew something that she did not. Whatever it was, she sensed a need to build an invisible wall around herself for protection. Perhaps not necessarily from the man himself, but more likely from Philip's expectations.

"Lady Northcott, how very nice to see you again," Daniel Morgan said in the most determinedly clipped tones Clarissa had ever heard.

"Good evening, Mr Morgan," Eliza said, turning to Clarissa. "My dear Clarissa, please allow me to introduce you to Daniel Morgan. He is new to this part of Cornwall," she added.

"I am pleased to meet you, Mr Morgan," Clarissa said with muted enthusiasm as she lightly bowed her head.

"And I am pleased to meet you too, Miss Tate," he said, and Clarissa felt that awful sensation in her stomach once again; *Miss Tate? But how did he know her full name?* She had not yet been fully introduced to him.

"I hope you find the Gribben Peninsula to your liking, sir," Clarissa spoke without thinking, using the ordinary platitudes of what passed for polite conversation in their society.

"I do not live on the Gribben Peninsula, Miss Tate. I have a house in Tywardreath," he said and gave her what she could only describe as an oily smile.

"Tywardreath is a very pleasing place," Clarissa said, wishing that this pristine man would quit her company.

And pristine he was, for she thought she had never seen any man so determined to be neat. His tailcoat was very fine indeed, a deep black with lapels of velvet. The collars of his crisp white shirt sat so high that she was humorously reminded of a Jacobean ruff. It seemed to make him impossibly long-necked and his physical stance somewhat proud and pompous. With a head held so high, she wondered if his muscles ached when he released himself from such binding.

To make matters worse, his silver-grey cravat was tightly done, holding those crisp collars up like wings about his chin. It was such a determined look that she couldn't help but compare him to Felix Ravenswood the first time she saw him. That slightly open shirt and the cravat; not worn as a cravat, but in the loose knotted style of a working man.

Felix's hair, dark, wavy, and overgrown, would have looked like an outrage on the top of Daniel Morgan's head. And that thick woollen waistcoat she had first seen Felix in, his shirt sleeves rolled up and his tanned forearms exposed to the elements were in stark contrast, and she could not imagine Daniel Morgan ever suffering such a style. And yet, despite Felix's appearance on that first meeting, she had sensed his quality, his confidence. There was something not quite right about Daniel Morgan, with his neatly clipped fair hair and strident standards in his mode of dress. Everything about him seemed forced, almost tense, despite the languid way he looked her up and down. Oh, how she would have given anything to spend this valuable time in the company of Felix Ravenswood. What a rare opportunity it would be to get to know a man whom she already realised was so very different from any other she had ever met.

"Yes, Tywardreath is very pleasing. And I am bound to say that you have a very fine home, Mr Morgan," Eliza said, unwittingly shattering the illusion that she barely knew him.

"Thank you kindly, My Lady," he said and performed a pathetically elaborate bow.

"Perhaps we should call on you, for I cannot bear to think of you all alone here, Mr Morgan," Eliza began as if reading from a script. "I simply cannot bear it."

"You are kindness itself, Lady Northcott."

"And which part of Cornwall do you hail from, Mr Morgan? You *are* Cornish, are you not?" Clarissa said, her own tone becoming a little clipped and interrogatory.

"Indeed, I am, Miss Tate. I hail from Bodmin," and there it was again, that oily smile.

"How pleasant," Clarissa said without a hint of enthusiasm.

The evening continued in that vein, with Clarissa doing everything in her power to be polite, but not too polite. To be attentive, but not too attentive. And, when Daniel Morgan asked to have his name pencilled onto her dance card, Clarissa claimed a headache. Her dance card was empty, and she regretted to inform him that it would have to remain that way for the rest of the evening.

Mr Morgan had taken the news with a self-assured smile and only the irritated glances exchanged between Philip and Eliza told Clarissa that she had not behaved in the manner they had hoped for.

Well, as far as Clarissa was concerned, they could just keep hoping.

Chapter Nine

The following week, after receiving a hastily scribbled note from Lady Marchmont, Clarissa attended Mrs Nancarrow's bridge game for the first time since the old Earl had passed away. She had wanted to get out of Northcott, for Philip and Eliza's attitude towards her had not only immediately returned to what it was before Lord and Lady Sedgwick's ball, but perhaps was now something falling even shorter of the mark.

Clarissa knew that she had angered them both by not tripping over her own skirts to dance with Daniel Morgan. It had hovered uninvited in her mind since that night, the idea that they had some design in introducing her to Daniel Morgan in the first place. Still, if it came to it, she would simply leave. Clarissa would find herself some respectable rooms, even if she would have to scrape by on her yearly allowance to have them. She would not be cajoled and bullied into marrying a man she had not chosen for herself; if, indeed, that was where the little piece of theatre the three of them had performed on the night of the ball was truly heading.

She liked Mrs Nancarrow very much, and she was certain that playing a little bridge would soothe her whirling thoughts. Not to mention the fact that Clarissa did not like to let Lady Marchmont down, especially since she had gone to the trouble of writing to her to implore her to attend. As for Philip and Eliza, Clarissa had not bothered to ask their permission this time. She was a fully-grown woman and emancipated to boot; to continually ask for permission would be to hand them her power entirely and that was something that Clarissa had decided against. She had decided against it the very moment she had seen Philip leading Daniel Morgan across the room towards her.

"I knew you would come, my dear," Lady Marchmont was hovering in the hallway of Mrs Nancarrow's large country mansion in Bodinnick, across the estuary from Fowey and overlooking that beautiful river on one elevation, and out to sea on another.

"And I am so pleased you are here, Miss Tate," Mrs Nancarrow added.

Clarissa smiled warmly and felt an immediate surge of fine spirits. The two ladies greeting her in the hallway so enthusiastically gave the distinct impression that they had been waiting there for her, both of them keen that she should come. In some little way, Clarissa felt as if the two older ladies had taken her under their respective wings. It was something that Lady Marchmont would make no secret of, but Mrs Nancarrow, a little quieter, a little staid, and at nearly sixty, a good deal older, was somewhat more subtle. And yet, despite their differences, the two ladies got along very nicely, and Clarissa found she liked them both a great deal.

"I am so pleased to be here, Mrs Nancarrow, thank you for inviting me. And Lady Marchmont, how kind of you to write to me. Really, I do believe I was in need of a little prompting and I thank you for it," Clarissa said, giving over her hands as Lady Marchmont reached for them.

"Well, let us go into the drawing room and have a little tea, shall we?" Lady Marchmont led her away.

"Enjoy yourselves, my dears. I have a guest or two left to greet," Mrs Nancarrow said, determined as always to make each and every one of her guests most welcome.

"I hope you do not mind, but I had Mrs Nancarrow extend an invitation to Felix Ravenswood. He has been here before, of course, but not for a long while." As Lady Marchmont spoke, Clarissa felt her heart begin to beat a little faster.

"He is here?" Clarissa said breathlessly.

"Yes, he is. I had thought about saying nothing and simply claiming the whole thing to be a wonderful coincidence, but you are too clever for that and I have no intention of secretly interfering," she led Clarissa by the hand to a little couch under one of the large stone-mullioned windows.

"So, this would be more of a bold and plain sort of interfering, Lady Marchmont?" Clarissa said, her amusement and excitement mixing together to form a heady brew.

"Exactly that!" Lady Marchmont said and laughed loudly, drawing one or two fierce glances from bridge players in deep concentration. "Oh, I do like you my dear, you speak your mind. You might do it in a quiet and somewhat more decorous way than I do, but you speak it nonetheless."

They settled down on the couch and made themselves comfortable, with Lady Marchmont looking hopefully around the drawing room to catch the eye of one of the maids. In no time at all, one such maid was walking towards them with a laden tea tray.

"Three cups, Lady Marchmont?" Clarissa said with a hint of sarcasm the moment the maid had left them. "It is as if the maid already knew."

"My goodness, you miss nothing, do you? Well, you are quite right, I have set the whole thing up."

"Oh no," Clarissa said, feeling suddenly embarrassed.

"Fear not, my dear, I did not make Felix part of my scheme. He is not privy to any of this," Lady Marchmont said jubilantly.

"Although I am sure he will see clean through it, will he not?" Clarissa laughed.

"Probably," Lady Marchmont shrugged elaborately.

Without another word, she looked across the room again and then waved a slim, pale hand. Clarissa followed her gaze, knowing that Felix Ravenswood would be on the other end of it, but still being surprised somehow to see him there.

He looked very smart in a navy-blue tailcoat and waistcoat with pristine black trousers and gleaming knee boots. He wore a white shirt and a dark blue cravat with a curiously casual ease which reminded her of the stark contrast between him and Daniel Morgan. Clarissa almost laughed to think of that proud young man with his head held forcibly high by his stiff collars.

When Felix began to walk towards them, Clarissa decided that it would simply be easier to let go of her internal resistance to the whole thing. Yes, there was an element of the embarrassing to Lady Marchmont's methods, but there was nothing that Clarissa could do about it. To concentrate upon the feeling would undoubtedly make her a little tongue-tied and a little flustered. With a man like Felix Ravenswood, she had the distinct impression that she would be far better off to brazen it out as if it was not all so terribly obvious.

"Tea for three, Gwen?" Felix said, when he was but three feet away from them.

"I must be losing my touch, Felix. Either that or I am surrounded by some rather fierce intellects," Lady Marchmont said and laughed as she patted the seat of the armchair set adjacent to their couch.

"Maybe it is both, my dear." He remained standing for a moment, turning his attention upon Clarissa. "Good afternoon, Miss Tate. I trust you are well?" he said and bowed before finally sitting; he had never bowed to her before and the small gesture, missing in their original meetings, seemed extraordinarily formal, rather than the commonplace greeting it was in society.

"I am well, thank you. And you are well, sir?" Clarissa was pleased that her voice sounded normal and her cheeks did not flush.

"Yes, I believe I am," he said and smiled at her.

His unruly dark hair had been tamed a little, tied at the back of his head with a slim black ribbon. There was something about that hair and the heaviness of his brows which made the neatness of his clothing seem strange somehow; pleasantly strange, as if two things working against one another had, in the end, worked perfectly.

"Ah, Mrs Nancarrow beckons," Lady Marchmont said, getting to her feet and darting away.

"I doubt the veracity of that assertion," Felix called after her, and Lady Marchmont turned just long enough to throw back a mischievous smile.

"I hope you realise, sir, that I had no part in this," Clarissa said, smiling to indicate that she was not at all cross with Lady Marchmont.

"Nobody ever does, Miss Tate, not as far as Gwen is concerned. But I suppose the thing I like best about her is that she never makes any pretence at subtlety. When I think of the many occasions on which I have suffered the presence of young ladies when their family, or mine, have decided that such a meeting would be fortuitous. But in such cases, everybody is pretending that is *not* the case; the meeting was quite a coincidence with no meddling hand stirring the pot. At least Gwen does not go that far," he looked across the room. "There is no sign of Mrs Nancarrow! Look, Gwen has managed to get herself a seat at one of the bridge tables."

"I have not known Lady Marchmont for long, but I like her very much. I must admit that I find her rather fun and that her company always goes some way to improving my mood. And I like her forthrightness."

"That is good, for there are many who do not. But that does not trouble Gwen, neither does it trouble her husband."

"They are both good friends of yours, I think," Clarissa said, wishing that she could broaden the conversation a little better; after all, had they not shared a most emotional and intimate moment?

They had been together as a soul had departed the earth and they had, in their own small way, being each other's only comfort. He had laid his hand on her head and gently stroked her hair and now they were sharing polite conversation over tea as if the last three months had somehow erased all of that.

"Very good friends. Gwen and Oliver Marchmont are sort of people who take the trouble to get to know a man for himself instead of taking the easier path and embracing idle gossip. I have been friends with them since long before I left Northcott Hall," he said, and Clarissa wondered once again what had caused him to leave.

"I think friends, real friends, are quite a rarity. Society is riddled with acquaintances, but friendship is quite something else, is not it?" she said and was pleased when he smiled and looked at her a little quizzically.

"It is an observation I have made myself." He paused for just long enough to take a sip of tea. "So, how are they treating you at Northcott now that my father has passed?" The question was surprisingly direct.

"I am certainly not ill-treated," she began tentatively. "I suppose the truth is that I am largely ignored, barely registering even as an inconvenience to my hosts."

"Hosts?" He said with a low chuckle.

"I truly do not know how else to describe Lord Northcott, if I am honest. He is not my guardian, he is not a relation, and I do not think that he particularly likes me. And, of course, the same holds true for his wife."

"If he is not your guardian, then who is?"

"Ah, had you attended the reading of your father's will, you would know," Clarissa said somewhat teasingly.

"Goodness, has he left you to somebody like some sort of an heirloom. Like a string of pearls or an unusual teapot?" He laughed heartily, drawing attention from the same determined bridge players that Lady Marchmont had unwittingly upset earlier.

"Teapot?" Clarissa said, her eyes widening with amusement. "No, have not been left in your father's will like an unusual teapot. Indeed, I have been left to my own devices. I have no guardian, despite my tender age." Finally, Clarissa felt that ease. "Your father declared me capable of autonomy."

Their acquaintance thus far had been unusual; combative initially, secretive, open with shared emotions, and then they had not seen each other for three months. She supposed that it was inevitable that the tiptoeing dance of polite society had not lasted long for either one of them as they sat drinking tea in a drawing room full of bridge players. It excited her; it reminded her of that day when she had teetered on the coastal path wondering if she had the courage to walk down into Smugglers' Cove to find him.

"I see," he said and nodded thoughtfully. "And are you relieved by it, or afraid of it?"

"Relieved," she said without hesitation.

"Very good," he said and nodded, his dark eyes studying her face.

"And what about you? How have you been since your father passed? I have not seen you since the funeral, but I did wonder how you were," Clarissa said, knowing that this was as personal a conversation she had ever had with a man before, barring her father and the old Earl.

"I manage much the same as I did, Miss Tate. I wonder sometimes what might have been, if there was something I could have done differently, but I suppose that is all by the by now," he said, once again studying her much more closely than polite society would ordinarily allow for. "Forgive me, I am a little amazed. I suppose because everybody else would assume that I did not care about my father and therefore would not think to ask."

"I both saw and felt your caring for your father," she said and then finally she blushed. "Forgive me, I ought not to have…"

"*Yes*, you ought to have," he said and laughed, a mixture of amusement and curiosity on that handsome face. "I am tired of people who never say what they mean and never mean what they say. Our class breeds them, does it not?"

"Perhaps I am not quite in your class."

"You are a baronet's daughter, are you not? As far as I can see, one title is much the same as another and all of them pointless," he laughed and shook his head. "I am afraid this is the real Felix Ravenswood, Miss Tate." he said in mock apology. "This is what makes the rumours so easily believed."

"Well, as long as you say what you mean and mean what you say," she said, parroting his words to great effect, for he laughed loudly once again.

Felix had been pleased and amused to receive the invitation from Mrs Nancarrow to attend the bridge afternoon. It had been a very long time since he had been a guest, the old standing invitation lapsing into obscurity over the years. But when Gwendolyn Marchmont had insisted, he had known that there was something to be seen, something of interest was going to happen. He'd idly wondered if it was a young lady, although he had not imagined that it would be Clarissa Tate. But now that he was sitting opposite her, listening to her speak and liking her way of saying things, he was glad.

She had crossed his mind more than once in the months since he last seen her. How could she not have? A young woman of such moral courage that she would defy a man who was soon to be Earl just so that she might do the right thing. And to do that right thing for a man she hardly knew was, in his opinion, even more courageous.

She was very young, barely nineteen and almost a decade younger than he was. Ordinarily, Felix did not find the company very young women particularly enthralling. They were either all nerves and impossible to talk to, or full of misplaced confidence and, as a consequence, equally impossible to talk to. They always found him handsome, he knew that. Handsome and a little bit exciting; forbidden. It was something he was far from flattered about; something he found rather tedious.

And yet he was quite certain Clarissa Tate thought him handsome too. He was not a conceited man or vain in any way; he knew he was a handsome man in the way that all handsome men knew they were. And perhaps the idea of Miss Tate finding him attractive was not as irksome as such situations ordinarily were.

"Be careful what you wish for," he said and laughed. "You might not like what I say, and you might like it even less if I mean it."

"I cannot see a downside to plain speaking, sir," she said, her thoughts seeming to flow freely into speech, no obvious attempts to impress him; nothing contrived. In fact, everything about her was very natural.

She was well-dressed, but plainly so, in a short-sleeved plum-coloured gown, its simple empire line having no sash or satin. She wore a tiny thin silver chain around her neck with a small locket hanging from it. He wondered if there was anything inside, for it was such a tiny locket. Her rich brown hair was coiled into a soft bun at the back of her head, one or two of her thick waves escaping to sit gently on her creamy collarbone.

Her brows were dark, framing her pretty hazel eyes, and her skin was young, clear, and with a natural rosy glow. In different clothes, such a healthy-looking young woman might well have been the daughter of a gentleman farmer rather than a baronet.

Somehow, the simplicity of her gown and hair made her natural beauty more prominent. Felix gnawed a little at the soft flesh of the inside of his mouth, as if to warn himself that such mental wanderings were not a good idea. She was a young woman, and in his experience, young women formed attachments very easily, quickly, and often deeply.

"Come to see me, Miss Tate. When you are out and about on your horse, drop down into Farwynnen Cove if you have a mind to," he heard himself saying, mildly unsurprised that his subconscious had taken over and ignored his more sensible thoughts. "If you are not too afraid to," he added for good measure.

"Afraid?" she said, but he could see a little something in her eyes which suggested a reticence.

Of course, it was likely only the ordinary reticence that most young ladies of their society could not escape, for it was so deeply ingrained.

"If you are not afraid to visit me alone. I can see I have made you uneasy, but I did not mean to. I am not predatory, I simply think that you are a little different and you might, if I am not greatly mistaken, have that little extra courage about you that is greatly missing in everybody else of either sex."

"That is a great compliment, sir," she said, and he knew she was thinking about it; she was playing for time.

"It is simply a fact as I see it, although I could be wrong. Nonetheless, you would be quite safe to call upon me for a few minutes whenever you were passing by on the coastal path."

"Then I shall very likely do just that, sir."

"So many people over the years have asked me why my father and I could not get along. I never answered any of them, and do you know why?"

"No, why?"

"Because I knew immediately that they were only asking as a means of satisfying their curiosity and nothing more. Even dear Gwen, although to a far lesser extent."

"And so, you have never discussed it with Lady Marchmont?" She began to look interested and much less cautious.

"No, I have never discussed it with anybody. You seem to be different, Miss Tate. We have twice been in the sort of situation in which that question might have reasonably been asked, and yet you did not. You do not seek to satisfy your curiosity as far as I can see, and you are the only person I have met who does not assume that I did not love my father. I think you see a situation, but you do not poke around in it; it is a rare thing indeed."

"Thank you," she said, and he was roguishly gratified to see her blush.

"Come to see me, Miss Tate. I think you are different enough to dare to call upon me. And if you do, then I shall tell you what stood between my father and I as far as I have ever understood it."

"I see," she said nodded. Felix was certain that she would come; absolutely certain.

Chapter Ten

Clarissa had woken several times in the night, each time mulling over every word, every pause, every part of their conversation. She knew that she would call upon him in the coming days; she had known it all along, there had been no internal struggle. It was not solely his declaration that he would tell her that which he had not, apparently, told anybody else, for she knew that she would have gone even without such an inducement.

There was something about him; he was the opposing pole, the magnet drawing her in somehow. Even as she lay awake staring at the little streaks of light the moon threw across the ceiling of her chamber, she knew she could not be entirely sure if such magnetism was a good thing. As far as her limited experience went, experience largely drawn from novels, magnetism was never anything but fierce. Fiercely wonderful, or fiercely disastrous. And yet still she knew she would go. She had not planned to go the very next day, but in the end, that is exactly what she did.

Coming down early for breakfast, Clarissa had quietly approached the dining room and overheard Philip and Eliza talking. She had slowed down, pausing some feet away from the partially open door, and looked over her shoulder. If she was to be an eavesdropper, she most certainly did not want to be discovered.

"Perhaps it would be simpler to invite him here first for afternoon tea." Philip's voice always carried, even when he spoke softly.

"Why? I have already begun to sow the seeds, have I not? Did I not mention at Lord Sedgwick's ball that we must call upon him? Surely, she will realise that I meant for her to go with me," Eliza said, sounding a little waspish, as if trying to hide her exasperation.

"You did indeed, my dear. I just sensed a little resistance in her that would be a little easier to overcome if Daniel Morgan were to come here instead. I think it would seem much more natural to have the man come here, ostensibly visiting us, rather than taking Clarissa over there and arousing her suspicions."

"Why should we care if her suspicions are aroused?" Eliza snapped.

"You forget, my dear wife, that I am not her guardian. She is emancipated, and there is nothing I can do about it. A final foolish act of a very foolish man, but there it is." As she stood listening, Clarissa felt her body grow tense with anger; how dare they speak of her that way?

"Emancipated she may be, but I wonder how she would feel about being suddenly without a roof! You must not underestimate the bargaining power you have, Philip. And when the time comes, you must not scruple to use it," Eliza said forcefully as Clarissa stood outside the door seething with every fibre of her being. "We must put ourselves first, Philip."

But as angry as she was, Clarissa was glad to have overheard the conversation. For reasons of their own, they wanted to throw her under the wheels of Daniel Morgan's carriage, so to speak, and she was far better fully informed than not. And since she had already decided to make her own way in the world should such a thing transpire, Clarissa smiled to herself; they may try all they wanted, they may throw in as much effort as they could muster, it would not come to pass. She was safe, and she gave a silent prayer of thanks to her father for leaving her enough of an annuity when the rest of the estate had been entailed away to a distant male relative. It was not a king's ransom, but it was certainly more than most young ladies could look forward to in her position. Her life would be very different, of course, and her reduced circumstances might well see her somewhat barred from the upper echelons of society. Nonetheless, if that was the price of freedom, then so be it.

Deciding there and then that she could not possibly sit down and eat with two such loathsome people, all the while trying to keep a tight lid on all that she had just overheard, Clarissa hurried noiselessly past the door. She hastened to the cloakroom where she knew she had previously left a lightweight shawl; just enough to keep her warm if the Summer sunshine deserted the day, as it so often did in England.

From the cloakroom, she hurried out of the main door, closing it gently behind her, and darted away down the stone steps. She crossed the lawn, heading around the side of the hall to the stables where she was greeted by the stable master himself. He had a warm smile for her, something he had in common with most of the Northcott servants. He saddled her horse in a heartbeat.

By the time she was ambling along the woodland pathway which would lead her out of the estate, Clarissa already knew where she would end up; Smugglers' Cove.

When she arrived at the place on the coastal path where she knew she would drop down to Farwynnen house, Clarissa slid out of her horse's saddle. She hovered for a moment, cautiously looking all about her across the Gribben Peninsular as far as she could see. As soon as she was sure she was not being observed, she led her horse down that steep path, her nerves overshadowed by her fear of being seen.

On her previous two visits, Clarissa had gone with purpose, a purpose which could have, if the worst had come to the worst, been explained. But the constraints of her upbringing and the world around her were not lost on her and she knew that there would be no explaining this. Something had made her believe Felix Ravenswood when he declared that he was not predatory, and she knew fine well that she herself had a very steady character, a character well deserving of the emancipation that her old guardian had finally allowed. Nonetheless, it was the view of others, the gossip, the way that almost everybody she knew would be so easily tempted to think the very worst. But was that not their own fault? Was that not their own failing? Of course, Clarissa knew that it did not matter; if such gossip flew along the south coast of Cornwall, her life would be miserable.

When she was halfway down the path, she could hear a sort of hollow and rhythmic banging. Making her way around the front of the house, she led her horse towards the stables, following the sound. When she reached the corner, she paused and peered down the side of the house, seeing that Felix had set himself up some little way past the stables and was chopping wood. Once again, he was in shirt sleeves, and they were rolled to his elbow. He had discarded his waistcoat this time, and there was a little roughness to him, a little something of the working man.

She continued to watch in silence, holding onto her horse's bridle and standing there a little foolishly. And yet she could not take her eyes from him, he was such a fine-looking man. With every swing of the axe, his overgrown dark hair flew and the muscles in his forearm tensed with the effort.

Despite the estrangement, he was still the son of an Earl. But as fond of the old Earl as she had been, Clarissa could not begin to imagine that the man had ever done anything like that. He was a man who had been raised to have servants take care of his every need and she was certain that he had barely done a thing for himself his entire life. Where had Felix Ravenswood developed his own instinct for self-sufficiency? And was he entirely self-sufficient? If he had servants, where were they now?

He rested the head of the axe on the large stump upon which he had been chopping the wood. He leaned his elbow on the wooden shaft and ran the back of his hand across his forehead before turning his palm and running his fingers through his thick hair, pushing it away from his face. Clarissa chose that moment to clear her throat, and he turned sharply to look at her.

"You did say to call on you, did you not?" she said and winced apologetically. "I apologise, I did not realise you would be so busy."

"I am not busy; I am just chopping a little wood." He smiled at her and she felt a little more at her ease. "But I will stop now, for a moment, come," he said and beckoned her with a wave of his arm. "Put your horse into the stable, Miss Tate, there is plenty of hay in there to keep him occupied."

Clarissa did just that, leading her horse into the neatly kept stable and watching for a moment as he nibbled contentedly on the corner of a hay bale. Content that he would not wander off, she walked back out to Felix.

"Perhaps you would rather sit outside for a while?" he said, and she realised that he thought to calm her nerves. "You have not only caught me at wood-chopping, but also at a very rough sort of meal," he laughed, looking at the plate of bread and butter which had been set on another cut tree stump.

Clarissa eyed the bread and butter, suddenly mourning the loss of the breakfast she had so hastily forgone. She looked back to see him smiling, amused.

"Would you care for a slice of my lowly meal?"

"Yes please," she said, pleased to see that she had surprised him. "I have missed my breakfast this morning and I usually eat rather well."

"Do you often miss your breakfast?"

"No, not as a rule," she said and reached out to take a slice of bread when he waved the plate in front of her. "Thank you," she said and immediately took a bite.

Although the bread was roughly cut and rather solid, it was very tasty indeed. Not quite the sort of thing one might find in a fine mansion, but just about the nicest she had ever tasted. Whoever had baked this bread surely had a talent for it and she began to wonder almost immediately just who it was who looked after Felix Ravenswood; who fed him? Who kept his house?

"I am glad you came, Miss Tate," Felix said, laying his discarded waistcoat over the tree stump he had been chopping wood on so that she might sit down. "I really was not sure you would come. I certainly did not think you would come so soon," he went on.

"You must not think that curiosity led me here, for it did not, not really," she began and watched him as he settled himself down on the other stump just a few feet away from her. "Although I will have to admit to something equally self-serving, for I find that I am on the run this morning."

"On the run? Sounds rather exciting, tell me," he said, taking a bite of bread and chewing it thoughtfully before giving her his full attention.

"I overheard a little conversation between Philip and Eliza this morning, and they confirmed something that I have suspected for some days now," she began. When he didn't speak, she continued. "And that is that they have some design in marrying me off to a man called Daniel Morgan."

"Marry you off?" Felix said and laughed in that hearty, unguarded way she had come to recognise.

Clarissa could hardly believe she was having such a conversation with anyone, and certainly not with someone of such recent acquaintance. She pushed away images of her father, who would have most certainly been disappointed to hear her discuss such private business with anybody, especially a stranger. He had raised her well, or at least he had raised her in the same style that everybody else raised their daughters.

"Yes," she said, knowing that she must continue.

After all, she already could not bear for him to think that she was simply nosy; an inquisitive young woman who was no different from the rest. It was true that she had been keen to know what had ruptured the relationship between father and son, but it did not consume her; she would not go to any lengths to secure such information. In choosing to tell her willingly, the truth was that Felix Ravenswood had paid her a wonderful compliment, and if he could take her into his confidence in such a way, why could she not do the same?

"This Daniel Morgan is a friend of theirs, is he?"

"He certainly seems to be, although I have never heard of him before and I am bound to say that Eliza tried to make light of it, as if they were barely acquainted."

"What makes you think they mean to marry you away?"

"It is a mixture of two things, really. The first one is, granted, a suspicion formed merely by my own observations, and that is the rather clumsy way in which they introduced him to me at Lord and Lady Sedgwick's ball," she began.

"Oh dear, Lord and Lady Sedgwick," he said and grinned ruefully. "A nice pair, really, but they do rather cling to their more illustrious guests."

"I think I have perceived the same myself," she said and smiled back.

"And what is the second thing?"

"Oh, that is much sturdier in terms of forming suspicions," she began humorously. "The conversation I overheard between Philip and Eliza was about inviting Daniel Morgan to afternoon tea in such a way as I would not be made suspicious."

"Ah, much sturdier, as you say," he was still amused. "But do they have such power? Even at your tender age, you no longer have a guardian. Who is there to tell you what to do but yourself?"

"Yes, that is very true," she said, pleased that he had come to the same conclusion that she had only an hour before.

"You are untethered, Miss Tate, are you not?"

"Untethered," she repeated the word almost to herself; what a wonderful way of putting it. *Untethered.*

"And being untethered is a great freedom, a most unusual one which I would urge you not to waste in a hasty marriage to a pasty-faced youth," he finished, his handsome smile broad, his ordinarily brooding dark eyes bright and amused.

"Solid advice, sir," Clarissa said, somewhat amused herself; how could something which had made her so angry that morning already be amusing to her? Surely Felix was the key to that. "But tell me, how did you know he was pasty-faced?"

"They always are, Miss Tate."

"But he is not a youth, I think," she went on in something of a teasing tone. "Being rather nearer to your age than mine," she concluded.

"It is good enough for me that he is pasty-faced, Miss Tate. The rest I am happy to concede." He was chuckling again, and it was so unusual. He was not a man who laughed much, she was certain of it. He had been so serious in their first meetings, but of course he would have been; she was a stranger to him then, a stranger bearing bad tidings. "Now then, I promised you an explanation of my circumstances, did I not?" he said, changing the subject altogether.

"You might well have promised it, but you do not owe it."

"If I felt I owed it, Miss Tate, I would not give it," he said and rose from his seat on the tree stump. "I really am a very poor host, as you can see. I am not visited by the best in society because they think I am profligate, and so I suppose one falls out of the habit of such niceties. But even I can see that to hand a carefully raised young woman a rough slice of bread with no plate and nothing to wash it down with is an offence by almost anybody's standards," he went on, laughing. "Surely you do not fear me now, Miss Tate?"

"Fear you? I am not sure that I ever did," Clarissa said, and realised that it was the truth.

She had feared meeting him in the beginning, it was true. Even that very morning, she had feared his mockery for having dashed to see him so soon. But she had never truly feared *him*. There was something about him which excited her and always had, and her excitement made her a little fearful. But Felix Ravenswood himself had not frightened her. That was not to say that she would wholeheartedly trust him, for perhaps even pernicious gossip had some basis in fact, but she was not afraid. "Why?"

"Because I would like to invite you into my house rather than have you sit here on my chopping block, as it were. I can offer you a better seat inside and a glass of sherry and I shall be at my very most civilised in every respect," he said and then held her gaze firmly, so firmly that she began to feel a little breathless. "In *every* respect."

Chapter Eleven

Clarissa was not quite sure what she had expected to see on the inside of that grey, forbidding building. Farwynnen house was still somehow beautiful to her, a sort of acquired taste that she had developed and held onto.

They walked in through the front door, that great wide wooden arch pushed back with ease by Felix to allow her admittance. She walked ahead of him standing uncertainly on an immense and somewhat faded rectangular rug on a dark wooden floor.

It was an entrance hall of sorts, although nowhere near as grand as the one at Northcott Hall. This was a far less fussy space, with dark wooden half-height wainscoting from which white painted walls extended to the high ceiling, the dark beams thick and exposed.

It was a large space, much larger than she had been expecting, and he stood a little to one side for a moment, saying nothing, as if giving her the opportunity to get to know it.

Her eye was drawn to two portraits, handsomely painted and displayed in round gilt frames. There was one either side of a wide stone fireplace, disproportionately wide for the size of the room, she thought. However, being almost on top of the sea must surely bring extraordinary draughts into the house.

"My grandfather and grandmother, Jago and Matilda Roscarrock," he said, his voice pleasantly informative, no suggestion that he thought her curiosity intrusive. And on the opposite wall, my mother, Morwenna Roscarrock," he went on, walking her over to the portrait, standing closely at her side as she studied it.

Looking into the face of the young woman whose portrait must surely have been painted when she was younger than Felix was himself, Clarissa could see where he had got his dark and irresistible looks. The young woman looking back at her was beautiful; truly beautiful. She had the same dark wavy hair as her son, only it roamed free over her shoulders, being only clipped back at the front. It gave her that slightly wild look that Felix had; perhaps not wild, but *free*. Her eyes were large, dark glossy pools of black ink, and her lips full and rosy. Clarissa knew that portrait painters were apt to err on the side of flattery, but she had no doubt at all in her mind that Felix's mother had been depicted with great accuracy. She looked so like Felix; how could it not be a true likeness?

"She was very beautiful, very beautiful indeed," Clarissa said, mesmerised by the portrait as she spoke in a near whisper.

"She was the finest of mothers. I was blessed to have her," there was a note of something in his voice that she couldn't place. "But she died a long time ago. My grandparents survived her, although my grandmother not by much. My grandfather passed almost six years ago now, an old man of such Cornish grit that I thought he would be here forever. He left Farwynnen to me, as if he knew that I would one day need it."

"You were a close family? Here, I mean, your maternal family?" She knew she was prying and yet, standing there in that large rectangular room with its arched windows and the sun's rays doing what they could to fade yet more of the red rug, the conversation felt right.

He was a strange, mysterious man. He was undoubtedly a mystery to many more people than just Clarissa, and yet he had chosen to invite her into his world. Just how far he intended to let her in, however, she couldn't say.

"A very close family, yes. My grandparents adored my mother, their only child, and they pleaded with her not to marry my father. Still, I am getting ahead of myself and I have yet to have you seated in comfort and given a drink."

He walked through the large room, Clarissa following along in his wake, and through a large stone archway which led into a wide corridor. Just a few steps along this corridor led them to a heavy wooden door which was partially ajar. Felix pushed the door open and stood back a little, holding out his arm to indicate that Clarissa must enter first.

She walked into another large room which seemed to serve two purposes. At one end, there was a couch and two armchairs, all covered in a thick, dark grey brocade. The furniture was old, but very fine indeed, and she could see that it suited its situation so well that it must surely have been made just for this house.

At the other end of the room was a large wooden dining table. It was made of great wide planks of the darkest wood, a long and narrow surface, despite its great thickness, which looked more like a great bench than a fine table one might see in Northcott Hall. There was a wrought iron candelabra at either end, each containing five candles, no prettiness to them and yet that strange, rugged, almost medieval beauty that fitted the house so well.

There were seats all around the table, and she could see that it would easily accommodate ten people, although she could hardly imagine that Felix Ravenswood entertained on that scale.

The floor of that large room was also of a thick, dark wood. Everywhere was dark, with that same wooden wainscoting to shoulder height and the rough walls painted white to the ceiling providing contrast. There was a chandelier hanging above the table, an impossibly heavy looking thing again made of wrought iron, again providing an unfussy and yet beautiful addition. Clarissa looked back down towards the sitting room area to see that there was an identical chandelier hanging there. She tried to imagine just how out of place such a thing would look at Northcott Hall, with its insipid, semi-fashionable perfection replicated from room to room. No, it would not fit at all; it would not look beautiful there.

There was another disproportionately large fireplace, set ready with kindling and logs. So large a grate must surely provide enough heat for the room, even on the coldest of Cornish winters. There was a tall candle stand on the floor by the fire, and she imagined the glow it would cast on a dark night.

Realising that they were at the front of the house, Clarissa walked to the line of arched windows, remembering how she had thought the building reminded her of an ancient church or a chapel when she had first seen it in its entirety. The windowsill was at chest height, and she rested her hands on its thick dark wood as she peered out at the Cove beyond.

"What a wonderful view," she exclaimed in breathless wonder. "I have a view of the sea from my own chamber at Northcott, but it is nothing like this. I see across the peninsula, of course, its undulating land, beautiful green grass, and the line of the sea above it, neat and distinct. But this is something else altogether; this is *alive*," she went on, staring out as the sea, calm and blue on that day, gently lapped at the black rocks of the cove. What a dramatic scene it must be on a wild Cornish day. "It must be the most wonderful view in all of Cornwall."

"I daresay there is many a Cornishman who would argue. We are all the same deep down, are we not? We all fiercely defend our own little plot in the finest of all counties," he chuckled.

"Do you prefer it here to Northcott?" she said, surprising herself with so direct a question.

"It feels like home, Miss Tate."

"And Northcott did not?"

"No, Northcott did not. In part I understand why, but the reason which lay behind it is something I have never understood," he said, striding across to a heavy wooden sideboard upon which sat a silver tray with a fine lead crystal decanter and glasses.

As he poured two glasses of sherry, Clarissa thought that this was a most beautiful and usual place. It was a large house, a house of some wealth, despite its darkness. This was not the home of an ordinary family, a working family with the same cares suffered by so many others in their part of Cornwall. Despite its ruggedness, its isolation, it was the home of the sort of people who had likely been invited into the same sort of society that she and her father always had. It was not the rampant wealth of Northcott, but wealth, nonetheless.

"Please, sit," he said, indicating the dark grey couch with a nod of his head.

As soon as she was seated, he handed her the small glass of sherry before taking one of the armchairs opposite her. He immediately took a sip of his drink, and she was reminded of Philip's snarling rumours of his brother's drunkenness. She was reminded of the day she had seen him stumbling out of Sir Hugh Trevithick's home in Tywardreath more than two years before. But a small glass of sherry was not such an unusual thing in any house, was it? Although perhaps not so usual in the middle of the morning.

"I am not a drunk, Miss Tate," he said, laughing. "But Bess Pengelly is not here today."

"Bess Pengelly?" she said, confused.

"My housekeeper. She is a married woman, and does not actually live here at Farwynnen house, but comes here every day to work. Unfortunately, her husband is not a well man and, once in a great while, she does not appear. I understand, of course, and know that I could not manage this house without her. Not when my grandparents had once had five servants in total."

"And apart from Mrs Pengelly, do you have no other help?"

"I am certainly not a poor man, by any standards. Well, perhaps I am a little poor by the standards of the Northcott estate," he laughed and set his glass of sherry down on the side table. "But like my maternal grandfather, I have never been keen to be useless. I am a man and I can chop wood, saddle horses, light my own fires and pour myself a drink. I can even make a pot of tea, if the situation demands it, although I have chosen sherry today as a far easier option. Had Bess been here, we would have had tea. I hope you can forgive my rough ways, Miss Tate."

"I do not think your ways so very rough, sir. In truth they are a little intriguing, even a little admirable, I suppose."

"I am not sure whether or not that is a compliment, but I think I shall choose to accept it as such."

"Of course," she said, giving nothing away and pleased when he narrowed his eyes.

"So, would you care to hear any more? Although you said I do not owe it, I wonder if in some way I do. You did me a great service in having the courage to come here in the first place; a greater service still when you let me into Northcott Hall in the middle of the night. You have looked after my father, as far as I can tell, in the years since your own father passed away. I think we both owe you a great debt, and perhaps an explanation of our circumstances as best as I know them might go some way to beginning to pay it."

"Please forget any ideas of being in my debt, for you are not. But I should like to hear whatever it is you care to tell me."

"Well," he said and paused for a moment, staring across the room.

"You said that your grandparents begged your mother not to marry Lord Northcott," she said, in part trying to help him and in part thinking that it was probably best to begin at the beginning.

"Yes, I did. My father, you see, was a widower. He had been married before, to Philip's mother," he said, studying her face intently. "I see that surprises you."

"It does surprise me," she said, feeling that nothing but honesty would do; no coyness, no tiptoeing dance. "I had no idea that you and Philip had different mothers. But of course, nobody ever spoke of it and I most certainly did not ask."

"Well, Philip is, as I am sure you know, four years older than I am at two-and-thirty. His own mother passed away when he was still an infant, not yet a year old, although the circumstances have never been told to me. I asked my father time and time again, but he simply said that she passed away. So, when Philip was a small child of three, my father decided to marry again."

"And he chose your mother?"

"*Chose* is probably exactly the word, Miss Tate. I do not think that he fell in love with her, or even regarded her particularly highly. She was just a young woman who was fit and healthy, ready to provide a spare heir I expect, from a good family of a class who might be surprised to marry into such a title, despite such things not being entirely unheard of."

"Is that what worried your grandparents?"

"No, they were very confident people, they had no pretensions, but they had no insecurities either."

"Then what worried them?"

"The fact that my grandmother, upon meeting my father for the third or fourth time, was certain that he would never love anybody but his first wife. Her fear was that he would come to resent the woman he had chosen to replace her, and that fear proved itself in the end."

"But your mother loved your father?"

"She was a young woman when she first met him, younger than you are now; of course she loved him. Young women always love, do they not? And they often love unwisely and far too deeply for their own peace of mind."

"I cannot say, but I expect that is true. What is the point in loving if it is not deep?" Clarissa said, speaking from the heart before she had a moment to temper words.

She could feel her cheeks blushing and she hastily lifted the small sherry glass to her face and took a sip. He was quiet for a long time and she wondered then what he thought of her; did he think her a silly young woman tripping over her own skirts to fall in love for the first time? Clarissa felt a curious urge to tell him that it was otherwise; to tell him that if and when she fell in love, she would know exactly what she was doing. But of course, that would simply make her seem so much younger and so much less experienced than she already was.

"I believe my mother must surely have felt the same way as you, for she was still so in love with him, even in her last days. It was a tragedy, a mistake, and one which I have struggled to forgive. He ought never to have married my mother; she was a young and beautiful woman and he should have left her be. He should have left her to lead a life, to find a man who would have loved her as much as she loved him."

"Surely he was not cruel to her? I know I have only been at Northcott for three years, but he was always so kind to me." Clarissa did not want to hear that the man who had been a father figure to her had ever had a capacity for cruelty.

"Not ostensibly cruel, no. He did not shout, disparage, or ridicule. He just ignored her, as if she did not exist on the earth at all. But it was that which killed her, I am sure of it. Without his love, my mother wilted like a cut rose. She became more and more insubstantial as time passed, and even I, such a young man then, could see it."

"That is so very sad. *Goodness*, that is sad," Clarissa said, putting herself in Morwenna Roscarrock's shoes, and not liking how they fit.

"I asked my father why he married her, why he had so selfishly made her life a misery, and he told me that he had not meant to. He said he had so much to make amends to Jennifer for, so much that he could not make amends for after her death, and it had affected him greatly."

"Jennifer?"

"His first wife. Philip's mother."

"And he never told you what it was he needed to make amends to Jennifer for, did he?"

"No, he did not. He said some things were better left buried."

"He had a secret," Clarissa said, her voice a barely audible whisper as she remembered the Earl's final days and how he had told her of some mistake in his past which had become a secret.

"Miss Tate, did he tell you?" Felix sat forward in his seat, his eyes dark and brooding, just as they had been on that first day. "Do you know what it was?" It sounded almost like an accusation.

"No, but I shall tell you everything he told me," Clarissa said, keen to unburden herself and return them to the easy, comfortable footing of just moments before. "Not long before he slipped into the unconsciousness that was not broken until you spoke to him, your father did say something about a secret. He told me that he had caused enough pain and heartbreak in his life, something which he seemed truly troubled by. He said that a mistake, when not acknowledged, soon becomes a secret, and that such a secret has the power to tear a family apart. But I promise you now, he never told me what that secret was. He never told me, and I did not ask, and although we do not know one another well, I think you know enough already to know that to be the truth."

"Forgive me, I do know it. I cannot imagine you asking my father to give you details of any kind. You would not press for such information, most particularly not from one who was suffering through his final days."

"No, I would not. And there is nothing to forgive. In your position, with so much in the past that is hidden, I would be equally fervent, I can assure you. I wish your father had let something slip in those final days for I most certainly would have told you. I would have told you to give you peace, whatever that secret might have been. For your father to have dwelled upon it in those last days tells me that some final confession had been on his mind and I have no doubt that he would have made that confession had he not fallen into unconsciousness. And it was just in that moment when he spoke your name; that is why I sought you out in the first place. He spoke your name, just your name, and something about it touched me very deeply. I knew that I would have to come here."

The conversation had become so serious, so personal, and Clarissa had the greatest and most oppressive sense that there was no way out of it. The range of emotions she had felt in the short time she had been at Farwynnen had exhausted her. Her heart was not used to such fluidity; the humour, the sadness, the hint of desperation she had seen in his eyes that she could almost feel, the heartbreak of his mother, a young woman whose deep love was never returned. It was all too much for a young woman who had been raised to keep her own emotions within a very narrow tunnel. She felt as if they were trying to break out of that tunnel now and spread themselves wide, into rumbling blue sea beyond.

She could easily imagine that Felix Ravenswood's mother had been one who felt things very deeply. She could easily imagine that Felix Ravenswood, despite his occasional rough manner, his partial withdrawal from society, was one who would feel things deeply too. Perhaps too deeply.

Her own excitement was back, but it was far less pleasant than it had been when first experienced. The little flashes of fear attached to it were larger, more easily perceived, and she wanted to be away from him. She wanted to come back to Smugglers' Cove, but Clarissa needed to be free for a while, to breathe, to think about everything they had talked about.

"Will you come again?" he said, as if reading her thoughts.

"Yes," she said, knowing with all her heart that she would.

Chapter Twelve

By the following morning, Clarissa had recovered entirely. She had slept without waking once in the night and came to rather late in the morning. By the time she had made it into the dining room, it was to find a footman and a maid already removing the serving platters.

They had been full of apologies, but she had assured them that the fault was all her own; she had overslept and that was all there was to it. Declaring that the food was cold, the maid had promised to ask the cook to make Miss Tate something fresh, but Clarissa would not hear of it. A little cold bacon and tomato and a somewhat chewy piece of toasted bread was most certainly not going see her off, an assertion which drew a brief snort of hastily stifled laughter from the young footman. They liked Clarissa; they were a little more at their ease under her gentle direction.

In the end, she had eaten rather well insofar as she had eaten a lot, despite its somewhat cold and congealed state. With a full night of sleep behind her and a full stomach, Clarissa decided that she would do something she had considered more than once previously, albeit secretly.

Ever since the old Earl had spoken to her of his secret, a persistent little thought had hovered in the darker recesses of her mind. She remembered his words, how he had told her that his diary was once his friend, but that her kind companionship had made him rely upon that friend less and less in his last years.

"I used to write everything down in my diaries, Clarissa. Years and years' worth of them in these attics."

Could it be possible that his secret lay up there, just ink on a page that was waiting to be discovered? He had told her that there were years and years' worth of diaries in the attics. She closed her eyes and remembered how he had lain in his bed, feebly pointing up at the ceiling as if to indicate the very place where they were. Of course, Clarissa knew that she could not really claim that it had been his way of giving her permission to poke about in the old details of his life, the innermost thoughts that a person generally committed to a diary. Things that he had not been able to speak aloud.

However, at the same time, there was something of which she was absolutely certain; the secret had troubled him, and had he maintained his consciousness, she was sure that he would have unburdened himself in the end. Perhaps even to Felix, the son he had asked for in the end, allowing him to live a life without secrets.

Even as she made her way through Northcott Hall, up the main staircase, along the corridor on the first floor where her own chamber lay, she wondered if she could really do it. It was true that a little eavesdropping, from time to time, was not entirely beneath her, but surely that was the same for almost everybody. But could she really sink to such a low point? And was it really a low point, or was it the only sensible way to help a man who had passed away and could no longer do anything to set things straight between himself and the son who did, as she very well knew, still love him?

She continued past her own chamber, all the way to the end of the corridor where a low and narrow wooden door led out onto one of the servants' staircases. She thought it the best way to get to the top floor of the house without being noticed. If she continued up the main staircase and was discovered, she would struggle to explain her presence on the floor above where Philip and Eliza kept their own rooms. And to continue higher still, surely there would be no explanation at all other than the truth; that she was making her way into the attics of Northcott Hall to snoop around.

Clarissa had not expected to cross paths with a servant at that time of day on the staircase but was still relieved to reach the door to the attic rooms without incident. She had never been in that part of the hall before. There were so many parts of Northcott Hall she had not seen and was certain that there were many parts she never would.

She turned the handle to discover that it was not locked, and pulled the door quickly open, stepping inside and closing it hurriedly behind her. She was confronted immediately by a single narrow flight of stairs, and she held onto the skirt of her gown, lifting it a little so that the hem did not drag in the dust she could see on each step. Surely nobody had been up here for a very long time, and there was some measure of comfort in that for her; a sense of solitude and safety.

Clarissa had put a candle and some matches in her pocket, but realised immediately that she would not need them. The vast attics stretched the full length of Northcott Hall, the small circular windows, although set a little distance apart, were just large enough and just regular enough to provide good light. She had never noticed the windows before, not from the ground below, and walked across to the far corner to peer out.

She had never been so high up in Northcott Hall and it felt somewhat vertiginous to look down now. The grounds below looked different from so high above, and she realised just how far she could see into the distance. Squinting, Clarissa could just make out the chimneys of Farwynnen House on Smugglers' Cove and she smiled to herself. She wondered if he was in there now, or if he was outside by the stable chopping wood.

Knowing that this would not get the task done, she turned away from the window and stared down the full length of the Northcott Hall attics. It was not as crowded with old furniture, hat stands, and wooden trunks as she had imagined, but it was far from empty. There were pockets of emptiness, clear spaces, interspersed with busy little areas full of all manner of things.

Hardly knowing where to begin, Clarissa thought that hat boxes and old wooden trunks would likely be the best bet. But which end of the attic to begin? Or should she begin in the middle? This was going to be a painstaking process, she knew that for certain.

It took Clarissa almost an hour of hurriedly searching through boxes and trunks in her end of the attics before she found anything of note. There was an old writing desk, a battered thing made out of fine mahogany. It was not until she had searched through everything else in that immediate area that it occurred to her to look inside.

She lifted the lid, but there was nothing more to see than the ink stained wood of the desk. She pulled open the little drawers one by one, relieved to find they were not locked. She had been about to give up hope of finding anything other than old pens and empty space when she found an old leather-bound book.

Clarissa drew it out of the drawer and opened it with hasty fingers, a gasp of victory escaping her when she recognised the old Earl's beautiful script. She thumbed through the pages and saw that each entry was dated; this was one of his diaries, no doubt about it.

But it was only one from a long life of writing, and Clarissa was keen not to leave the attic without at least two or three. The search continued, and although she was beginning to grow hungry, her cold breakfast already a distant memory, she determined not to stop until she had found some more.

It was another hour before she found three more little volumes further down the attics. They had been stored in the bottom of a well packed wooden trunk; one she had almost given up searching before the same leather binding caught her eye. She had four diaries now, that would be enough to begin.

Clarissa crept back down to her end of the attic, careful not to make a noise that might be heard on the top floor beneath. She was certain that there would be nobody there, for the third floor was used largely to accommodate guests when Northcott hosted an event of some magnitude. Nonetheless, there was no sense in being anything other than cautious.

With Felix still lurking in the corners of her mind, Clarissa could not resist a final peek out of the small round window. Setting the diaries down on the top of the old writing desk, she crept across to the window and peered out. She looked immediately for the chimneys, almost wishing she could see smoke rising from them. But it was a warm summer's day and she had a feeling that Felix was the sort of man who did not need a fire for anything other than truly inclement weather. Still, it would have been nice to see, to imagine him sitting there in that great, dark room on one of the grey brocade-covered chairs enjoying a small glass of sherry.

She shook her head; what was it about that man which so obsessed her? She had been about to turn away from the window when a movement closer to home caught her eye. She stood on tiptoe and craned her head to get a better look, peering down at what she realised was the side of the stable block. How different it looked from up here!

But there had been movement right enough and it was not, as she had expected, one of the stable lads. No, it was Philip Ravenswood himself, standing at the side of a horse she did not recognise whilst another man prepared to climb up into its saddle. Even from the back, the man was familiar to her. She might not have met Daniel Morgan more than once, but she would recognise that stiff collar induced stance anywhere.

What on earth was he doing here? Surely, he had not been invited to afternoon tea already. But that did not make sense, for while she did not exactly know the time, she was certain that it could not be far past midday and almost three hours before afternoon tea was customarily served Northcott, that was certain. Furthermore, Daniel Morgan looked more like he was leaving rather than arriving.

Whilst Clarissa did not particularly care, whilst she was relieved that she was simply looking at him from the attic and not in his dreadful company, still there was something there to concern her. There was something between those two men that she did not understand, and yet she knew that she formed a part of it. With nothing more she could do but watch him ride away and Philip stride towards the house, Clarissa knew that she would keep it in mind; she would not forget it. This was important somehow, even if she had no idea why.

With an unwelcome feeling in her stomach that could not easily be blamed on hunger, Clarissa took the four little volumes from the top of the writing desk and carefully stowed them away, two in each pocket of the skirt of her plain faun-coloured gown. It would not do to be caught on the servants' staircase with them in her hands, after all.

Clarissa made it back to her own chamber without crossing paths with a single soul and found that she was a little breathless with the clandestine excitement of it all by the time she had closed the door behind her and leaned heavily against it.

As keen as she was to begin searching through the diaries immediately, she knew she must not indulge herself, not yet. Clarissa needed to find a suitable hiding place for them, even though she very much doubted that either Philip or Eliza would ever have cause to come into her chamber. But this house was full of servants, and as much as she liked them all, the only one she could be certain of was Flo Pettigrew, and Flo Pettigrew was *not* one of the maids who made the beds and dusted the windowsills.

In the end, Clarissa found a loose floorboard, one which had, in years gone by, been cut short for some reason. She tucked her slim fingers into the gap as best she could and lifted it, smiling when she found an unencumbered little space beneath. She gently placed the four little volumes there and covered them up again, knowing that she would soon come back to them.

For now, she must wash the dust from her hands and face and change her gown before anybody happened upon her and wondered what on earth she had been up to.

Chapter Thirteen

"You do 'ave a visitor, sir!" Bess Pengelly said in the slow Cornish tone he always found soothing.

It reminded him of the way his grandmother had spoken; a woman raised in a fine enough house but being of a time when accents had been local; authentic, *real*. Women of his grandmother's class now adopted the tones of the truly upper-class, clamouring for the acceptance of those they saw as a little above them, rather than cherishing those they thought below, as well as their own heritage.

"Well, this is an exciting day indeed," he said, barking a laugh which surprised his housekeeper into wide-eyed silence; he was not always the most jovial of masters, even though Bess Pengelly knew him well and liked him well.

"I 'spect that might well depend on who it be trotting down the path, sir," she said, her simple bluntness always welcome and always amusing.

"You are right as always, Bess." He rose to his feet from the chair he had spent an enjoyable hour sitting in to read and began to make his way out of the room.

"Well, are you to answer it yourself, sir? Tedn't right, sir, not with a servant in the house," Bess sounded scandalised and he laughed; he loved the way she unfailingly replaced *isn't* with *tedn't*, it reminded him of his childhood.

"Bess, you are true wonder, and most spectacularly feudal, my dear," he said, laughing.

He knew the true source of his good mood, for Felix was certain that the visitor must surely be Clarissa Tate. Even Gwendolyn Marchmont did not call upon him unannounced, or indeed ever, for she did not like the look of the steep path down. To call speculatively was something he had only ever invited Clarissa Tate to do.

"I'm sure I don't know what you mean, sir, but I do reckon if I did, I wouldn't like it much," Bess said, with a look in her eye which suggested she might swat him like an errant child.

"It is a compliment, I assure you," he hedged his bets and smiled at her, keeping step with her as she determinedly made her way to the door in a bid to reach it first.

"Well, who is to open it, sir, thee or me?" She was getting exasperated with him now, and it only served to amuse him all the more.

"Thee, by which I mean me," he said, reaching for the handle and opening the door sharply.

"I suppose you'll be wanting to make the tea yourself too, sir, will you?" Bess said sarcastically.

"No, I think there my interference will end," he laughed, looking out as he excitedly waited for Clarissa to appear.

"Then I suppose I should thank the Lord himself for small mercies. I still have a job to perform 'ere in this house," she said, but made no move to head for the kitchen to prepare tea; no, Bess Pengelly was determined to see who it was who had her master suddenly full of foolish spirit and he knew it.

"Miss Tate, what a nice surprise," he said with bright politeness.

"I do hope it is not an inconvenience, sir, for me to call upon you so unexpectedly." she said, and he could see that she carried a small leather bound book in her hands.

"It is not an inconvenience at all, is it, Bess?" He turned to his housekeeper who was making a fine study of the young woman hovering awkwardly outside.

"No, it is not; not at all," Bess said, brightening when Clarissa smiled at her. "I must explain to you, Miss, it tedn't the sort of house where the master opens the door for himself. Not unless I'm not 'ere, of course, then he do 'ave to."

"I understand perfectly, Mrs Pengelly," Clarissa said warmly and Bess, delighted that the fine young lady already knew her name without them being introduced, forgot her annoyance immediately and beamed.

"'Tis only the master fooling with me," she went on. "Now, I must be off to the kitchen and get the tea a-brewin." And with that, she waddled away.

"Do come in, Miss Tate," Felix said, standing aside to let her pass through into the entrance hall.

"Thank you," she said and walked in, crossing the rug and allowing her eyes to stray to his mother's portrait.

He said nothing; with a tale such as the one he'd told her when she had last called, who would not be curious? Who would not feel compelled to look up into the oil-paint eyes of a long-dead woman, especially one who had died of a broken heart?

Felix had thought of Clarissa more than once in the days since he had last seen her. He wondered if she had recovered, for he had known she had taken everything he had told her right into her heart. He had seen how her beautiful face had paled that day, how the rosy glow of health deserted her in favour of taut emotions.

It had all left Felix wondering if she would ever come back. He had known her to be kind and caring, even courageous, from the very first moment he had met her. What he had not realised, however, was that she was one of that rare breed of women whose empathy for others was so strong that she felt the emotions as her own. And when she had said that there was little point to love if it was not deeply felt, he had not been at all surprised. He had, however, realised from that moment on that he would have to be very careful indeed. She had done him the greatest kindness, and at great risk to herself; he could not repay her by playing games with that tender heart.

Nonetheless, he could not deny the excitement he had felt when Bess had declared her arrival; even now, he could not quite get on top of it.

"You have brought me a book to read?" he said and laughed. "Perhaps you are going to read it to me? I am greatly intrigued."

"I do not know whether I ought to do either, if I am honest." Despite the cheer that her first meeting with Bess Pengelly had brought her, he could see seriousness creeping into her countenance.

"Well, perhaps you should sit down and see if that helps," he smiled, leading her into the drawing room with the smallest sense of foreboding lapping at the edge of his consciousness.

As she settled herself down, Felix studied her. Could she possibly be growing more beautiful by the day, or was it simply that his regard for her was growing? Once again, she wore a very simply cut gown, this time in a russet colour. With her clear skin and gleaming brown hair, perhaps there was not a colour in creation which did not suit her.

As she sat, she laid the small volume on her lap and stared at it as if she had a great weight of worry on her mind and that little book lay at the very centre of it.

"Your father kept a diary, sir. I do not know if you already know that, but I am a little nervous and I am afraid that I must begin somewhere." Her words came out in a rush, almost tripping over each other in their determination to be spoken.

"I have a recollection of it, although I do not ever remember him sitting down to write." He wondered where this conversation was leading.

"I never saw him sit down to write either, sir, but he told me in his last days that his diary had been something of a friend to him over the years. He even pointed to the ceiling as he lay in his bed and told me of the volumes and volumes which were in the attics above." Her cheeks flushed violently red and she looked chagrined. "I know that does not excuse what I have done, and I should not blame you at all if you are angry with me."

"You have found my father's diaries?"

"Yes. Not all of them, just a few." She paused and took a handkerchief from her sleeve, gently dabbing at her throat with it. "I realise that the Earl did not expressly give me permission to look simply by telling me where they were, and I realise further still that my behaviour is abhorrent, but please understand that I did not do it out of idle curiosity or anything but good intentions."

The air was heavy, as if an invisible cloud hovered thickly between them. Felix knew that it was largely his doing, for his heart was trying to catch up with his mind as he fought to discover exactly how he felt.

At that very moment, Bess came bustling in with a tray, the teacups clanking against one another as she went. She set it down on the side table and turned to Felix.

"Shall I pour it, sir, or would you rather wait until it be stewed a little better?"

"Let it stew, Bess," he said and laughed, the appearance of his unintentionally amusing housekeeper somehow snapping him out of that confusing little spell.

"Thank you, Mrs Pengelly," Clarissa said with a smile.

"You're welcome, Miss," Bess looked like the cat who'd got the cream before she made a small performance out of curtsying, a thing she never did, and hobbling away, the uncustomary movement clearly interfering with her well-worn old hip.

"Sir?" Clarissa said, prompting him gently; her eyes wide and a little fearful, and he knew he must put her out of her self-imposed misery.

"Yes, do you think you could call me *Felix*, my dear? I have enough with Bess and her *sir-this-and-sir-that* from daybreak until dusk," he said and was pleased to see the relief on her face. "We are friends, are we not? Our friendship may have been made quite suddenly, but the events of its earliest days are surely enough that we cannot think ourselves vague acquaintances."

"Yes, of course. You may call me Clarissa, if you wish it,"

"I do wish it, Clarissa," he said and smiled at her broadly, almost humorously, even as his insides swirled in apprehension. "So, you have found something in this diary?" He nodded at the book on her lap.

"I have not discovered any secrets, it is true. You must understand that *secrets* are what I was searching for. It is presumptuous of me, I know, but I wondered that, if you had a real answer for your father's behaviour towards your mother all those years ago, the knowledge might bring with it a little peace. I do not know, of course, and I wonder now if I ought to have asked you first before I had even begun to look."

"If you can find an answer to the question which I had asked my father over and over again, year upon year, with no response, then I am ready to hear it. I am ready to hear it whatever it is, however thunderous my countenance might appear, however abrupt my words might seem on occasion. You are the messenger, Clarissa, and I shall not shoot you. In truth, I think it is extraordinarily kind of you to have devoted your time to my future well-being, however unusual your approach." He laughed. "Cheer yourself, I really will not shoot you."

"Well that is a relief, at least," she said and relaxed. "How stewed is this tea going to get before it is to your liking, Felix?"

"Certainly, stronger than anything you are used to, I would wager. Still, let us pour it now and lessen the effects," he smiled as she put the diary to one side and set about pouring them both some tea; she added a little milk to his, and a great glug of it to her own.

After she had taken a sip, wincing a little at the strength of the brew, she set her cup and saucer back down onto the tray and lifted the diary.

"I have hastily read through four little volumes and, if I am honest, have found nothing that would help in a quest for the truth. But I did find something of importance, something which I thought you ought to see," she said, opening the diary to where she had placed a clean folded handkerchief between the pages.

"You read it," he said and set his own cup down, leaned his head against the high-back of the armchair, and closed his eyes.

"Very well," she said and cleared her throat.

"1ˢᵗ August, 1809.

The sun shines brightly on this day, but my heart is full of darkness. I have lost my son. Not to death, not to a wife, not to anyone or anything else. I have just lost him, and I know it is my doing. His anger is too great for him to suffer my proximity another moment, and I do not blame him for that. My heart is broken to see his confusion, to hear his questions and never, ever answer them. It is right for any child to love their mother, to be so loyal that they cannot bear the sight of the spouse who broke her. And I did break Morwenna, even though I had never intended to.

She deserved better in this world, and so did Felix. He was forced to choose between loyalty for his dearly departed mother, and whatever vestiges of feeling he still has left for the father who will love him until his dying day. But what good is my love when my truth has been lacking? What right do I have to happiness of any kind? It has been a long time, a very long time, since I could have claimed such thing as my right.

The only thing which holds my heart in my chest is the fact that he has not gone far. He is less than two miles from me as I sit at my desk; we exist still on the same peninsula, almost in the same place. But it is not mere topography which separates us, and I know that. I know it as well as I know this is all my fault, that Felix is yet one more victim of the lie. My lie.

Perhaps it is fitting that I can get no peace, that sleep evades me, and that I write these words in the dead of night while all of Northcott is asleep. All I can do is pray that my dear boy now sleeps, suffering nothing more than sweet dreams and a sense of peace. It is the very least he deserves. The very least."

When she finished, neither one of them spoke for some moments. Felix had his eyes closed, feeling the hot sting of tears he had not been expecting, and suffering the greatest anxiety that they would fall and, worse still, that Clarissa would see them. Friends they might now be, but he did not want to be diminished in her eyes. And so, he began to speak, keeping his eyes closed as he did so, waiting patiently for the unexpected emotion to pass.

"Thank you, Clarissa," he said, his voice most determinedly steady.

"I was very moved by what I had read, Felix, and I knew that you must see it. I hope I have not done the wrong thing."

"No, not at all. Not for a moment," he said, and began to feel a return to himself.

"So, shall I continue in my search? If I find something more, do you really want me to bring it to you? If you do not, I shall quit my search immediately. As I said before, I do not seek to satisfy my own curiosity."

"Continue your search. Bring me anything you find. I am ready to hear it, I meant what I said."

"Very well," she said and reached for her cup and saucer once more.

Chapter Fourteen

Over the next few days, Clarissa made regular but brief visits to the attic. Her nerves were lessening in this respect, but she did not want to be complacent. Such complacency could so easily lead to discovery, and she was most determined now to find an answer for that handsome, strangely beautiful man.

Clarissa did not bother to deny her attraction to him; it was an attraction she had felt from the start, from the very minute she had stared up at him, stuttering her purpose. But that had merely been an attraction to his somewhat wild, somewhat windswept appearance. It was a shallow thing; a girlish favouring of an extraordinarily handsome man.

Her attraction had grown greatly since then, and she knew it to be an attraction for Felix Ravenswood, the man. He was by turns mysterious then open, stern then amusing. He kept himself out of some society, and yet made himself most amenable to others. Clarissa had never met anybody like him in her life, neither man nor woman, and his was a character that she was drawn to, that she wanted to know more about.

Clarissa had discovered two more volumes of the old Earl's diaries in her latest little mission to the attics, disappointed that the last three she had looked through had borne little fruit. Having high hopes of these, or at least a bright sort of optimism, she tucked them away in that secret place beneath the floorboards. She would not get to them that day, for there were to be visitors to Northcott Hall and there was no means or sensible reason for her to escape their company.

There was an early evening buffet to be held in the drawing room, an affair that was neither formal nor informal. It was in that strange wasteland in between, where nobody seemed to know quite where they stood. It was the sort of event that ladies found it impossible to dress for, and men struggled to find the right tone in conversation. Clarissa much preferred either a formal dinner, or an informal breakfast when the hall was filled with staying guests. What a complicated set of circumstances England had weaved for herself! Even Cornwall, hardly a part of England at all, had not escaped it. No wonder she admired Felix; she was, she thought, a little envious of his freedom. But then was she not free herself? Untethered. It was still an idea she had to grow familiar with.

"Untethered," she whispered to herself, smiling at the very feel of the word Felix had used to describe her.

She rose from the floorboard, knowing that it was time to get changed, for she had much to do. She pulled the bell for assistance, having already asked Flo Pettigrew to expect such a call.

Within an hour, Flo had her mistress ready. She was not a lady's maid per se, but she was very skilled in dress and hair, and more importantly, Clarissa adored her.

"Are you looking forward to the evening, Miss?" Flo said conversationally as she put the finishing touches to Clarissa's hair.

"Not entirely, if I am honest," Clarissa said, knowing that to be honest with this particular maid would cause her no injury whatsoever. "There are several guests, which I ordinarily like because it gives a little variety and an occasional mode of escape if you are trapped with somebody for too long. But there is one person coming this evening who I have not yet been able to take to."

"Oh dear, is it the Captain of the Militia?" Flo said and winced at Clarissa's reflection in the mirror.

"Oh no, I have never yet been introduced to Captain Boscowan, no. It is somebody else altogether; a man called Daniel Morgan. Have you heard of him?"

"I'm afraid I haven't, Miss," Flo said as she slid another securing pin into Clarissa's thick hair. "Is he not pleasant, Miss?"

"Oh, he is very pleasant. Extraordinarily pleasant, Flo," Clarissa laughed a little wickedly. "So pleasant, in fact, that he cannot possibly be truly pleasant at all."

"Ah, you do not trust him, Miss?" Flo said confidentially.

"I do not trust him, and I most certainly do not trust His Lordship."

"Well, I know it is none of my business, Miss, but never forget that nobody can force you to marry. Not now."

"How clever you are, Flo. Already you perceive my real reason for not wanting to spend time in the company of Mr Daniel Morgan. Yes, I really do believe that the Earl has some plan to marry me to him. I cannot be sure of it, of course…"

"And you know me well, Miss. You know I shan't speak of it outside of this chamber."

"Of course, Flo. You are a good friend to me, my dear," Clarissa said and smiled at Flo in the mirror.

By the time she arrived downstairs, just as the guests were beginning to appear at the front of Northcott Hall, Clarissa was very suitably turned out for the event. She wore a lightweight cotton gown with long sleeves so that she did not have to agonise over whether or not long white gloves would be suitable for an event that was not quite so formal. Even *she* had those little concerns from time to time.

The gown was soft, a dusky pink colour which felt fit for Summer even though the sleeves were long. There was a narrow band of satin ribbon beneath the empire line, gently dividing the top of the gown from the bottom. The cut was simple, for Clarissa had never been comfortable in elaborate styles, nor even elaborately embroidered fabrics, but the colour suited her well and she felt both properly dressed and confidently comfortable all at once.

"Here you are!" Eliza said in a hiss when Clarissa descended the stairs. "I had begun to think that you were going to keep to your chamber all night."

"Forgive me, Lady Northcott, I had not thought I was late," Clarissa said, smiling politely but having no intention whatsoever of buckling, of silently seeking for permission to exist from a woman she could not abide.

"Well, wait in the drawing room for the rest of the guests. It is for Lord Northcott and I to greet people, after all," Eliza added when it was clear that Clarissa was not late at all.

Clarissa walked away without a word, smiling a little to herself at the foolishness of a woman who felt the need to dismiss another of her sex; to remind her that she was not a part of the family. It was on the tip of her tongue to tell Eliza that since the Earl had died, it was not a family she cared to belong to. More and more, the idea of some little rooms somewhere in the county seemed very appealing.

The first of the guests to arrive was none other than Captain Boscowan, the man she and Flo had talked lightly of earlier. He wore his red regimental jacket, the fine gold thread and golden buttons absolutely immaculate. The Captain was a man in his middle fifties who already had a shock of thick snow-white hair. The hair, however, was the only concession to age, for he looked as broad, upright, and vital as a man of five-and-twenty.

"My dear Captain Boscowan, allow me to introduce you to Miss Clarissa Tate. She was the late Earl's ward, and still resides here at Northcott," Eliza could not keep the tone of annoyance out of her voice, and Clarissa rather thought that the Captain had noticed it also, for his mouth turned up a little in one corner and his eyes, as he bowed to Clarissa, held hers and looked highly amused.

"What a pleasure to meet you, Miss Tate," the Captain said.

"And it is a pleasure to meet you too, Captain Boscowan," Clarissa said, and had a sense of already liking this man.

He had a refined sort of accent, but his Cornish burr was still discernible, and she felt lulled by it; soothed by it. Very much like the young Dr Morton, whose regional accent the old Earl had snobbishly, if humorously, disparaged, Clarissa could have listened to him speak all day.

"Forgive me, Captain, but I must re-join my husband for a moment to greet the rest of our guests," Eliza said, fluttering like a butterfly around a lettuce patch.

"Of course, My Lady," the Captain said and bowed, quickly turning his attention back to Carissa as his hostess wafted from the room. "Have you lived here long, Miss Tate?"

"But three years, Captain. I became the last Earl of Northcott's ward when my father passed away."

"I am so sorry to hear about your father, Miss Tate. But the Earl was a very fine man, and a fine guardian too, I should not wonder."

"Yes, he was very kind to me, and I have missed him these last months."

"You are from Cornwall originally though, are you not?"

"I am; Newquay, to be precise."

"There is no trace in your accent, Miss Tate, but I think one Cornishman can sense another. Or sense a Cornishwoman in this case, forgive me." He had such a nice face, such a nice smile, and his eyes were all ease and shining amusement.

"There is nothing to forgive," Clarissa said and laughed. "And you are right, we Cornish have a sense for one another."

"There are many guests to come this evening, are there?"

"Not too many, Captain Boscowan. Lord and Lady Sedgwick, who I am sure you know," she said and began to count the guests on her fingers as the Captain nodded thoughtfully. "Dr David Morton; he is our nearest doctor, being in Fowey, and a very clever man who took great care of the Earl in his last illness. Oh yes, Mrs Ariadne Parker-Wentworth and her niece, Miss Jane Penhaligon; very nice ladies indeed," she went on and he nodded. "Oh, and Mr Daniel Morgan, who currently lives in Tywardreath but is originally from Bodmin," she added as an afterthought, his relative geography the only thing she could think of to recommend him.

"Bodmin; I have not been there for some time, but it does bring back memories," the Captain said and laughed.

"Dare I ask if those memories are good or bad, sir?" Clarissa said, enjoying the conversation and already feeling entirely at her ease with the military man.

"A mixture of the two, I think. When smuggling was rife here in Cornwall, my younger years of service in the Militia were spent trying to track down the many hides that beautiful place contained. So many hides, Miss Tate, that I daresay we did not find but one-tenth of them."

"Of course, Bodmin was probably a very good place to choose; somewhere to hide the contraband before it made its final trip up-country," Clarissa beamed; she knew a little of local history and was pleased to have someone to talk about it with.

"They were very different times, though," he added solemnly.

"There are not many smugglers left today, I understand," she said, vaguely aware of the other guests arriving but keen to continue her conversation with the Captain and leave them all to find their own amusement.

She could vaguely hear Eliza's nasal exclamations drifting across the large drawing room, but she did her best to let them drift through her rather than let them sit heavy within the walls of her skull.

"Smuggling is a very different thing today, Miss Tate, but it still exists. In fact, it is the very reason that our soldiers are back on this particular coastline."

"My goodness, I suppose I am a little surprised by that."

"Oh yes, smuggling still goes on, Miss Tate," the clipped tones of Daniel Morgan surprised her, and she turned sharply to look at him.

"Indeed," she said flatly and saw the amused tilt of Captain Boscowan's mouth once again; he was probably a very good judge of character, for he had certainly already worked out Clarissa's likes and dislikes and she had not even said a word about them.

"Perhaps a young woman such as yourself thinks the whole thing very romantic," Daniel Morgan went on, giving her that dreadful oily smile, patronising her and undoubtedly thinking that he paid her a great compliment.

"I do not believe that smuggling has ever been a very romantic pastime, Mr Morgan. Recent history tells us that the people of Cornwall smuggled by necessity, even if it was against the law."

"Oh dear, know a thing or two about it, do you?" He laughed, throwing his head back as best as his unforgivingly high collars would allow. "Oh, do tell," he said, and she realised he was the sort of man who thought that a young lady was always impressed by allegedly superior knowledge most often displayed by laughing over whatever the lady said and explaining things to her very slowly; she liked him less and less.

"It is hardly a secret that the duties imposed by the government in London in the latter years of the last century made life in Cornwall impossible," she began, encouraged by an almost imperceptible nod from the very appealing Captain Boscowan. "Everybody on the Cornish coast knows of the importance of the pilchard catch. Perhaps it is less important in Bodmin, I do not know," she added, barely disguising her disdain. "But here in this part Cornwall, livelihoods depend on it and, as such, lives. When the government imposed such duties on imported salt that the Cornish could not afford to pay it, they were left with a very dubious and unenviable choice; smuggle or starve. Of course, in most recent years, those duties are no longer so onerous, and salt, brandy, and tea no longer luxuries. Smuggling has nothing to do with need anymore and everything to do with greed."

"Oh dear," Daniel Morgan said and gave a brief burst of braying laughter, presumably to hide his dismay at her knowledge.

"Indeed, that is right, Miss Tate. Neither scenario is romantic, and it most surely is greed and not need which drives the smuggler today." Captain Boscowan smiled broadly, looking almost proud of her. *"Greed and not need,"* he went on. "What a very good way of putting it, Miss Tate."

"My dear Clarissa, may I see you for a moment?" Eliza appeared suddenly at her side and took her gently by the arm as both the Captain and Daniel Morgan bowed politely to release her.

By the time Eliza had propelled her across the room, she no longer held her arm gently, but pinched it so hard that Clarissa was relieved to be wearing a long-sleeved gown, for a bruise must surely have already formed.

"Eliza, take your hand off me," Clarissa said in a low and dangerous voice, a voice she had never spoken to anybody under the roof of Northcott with before; her informal address had been instinctive too, for no *Lady* behaved in such a way.

Eliza let go of her immediately, so quickly that it was almost as if she had been burned. Her eyes were wide, and she stumbled over her words before finally forming an intelligible sentence.

"My dear, our company is not at all interested in hearing you talk about smugglers," she said in a whisper.

"Forgive me, Lady Northcott, but it was Captain Boscowan who initiated the conversation and indeed Mr Morgan who wanted to hear a little more."

"He was laughing at you, Clarissa, and rightly so. Men do not like young ladies who think they know more than they do."

"Lady Northcott, I do not *think* I know more than Daniel Morgan does; I *know* it," and with that Clarissa turned sharply on her heel and walked away.

As she began to cross the room, she was waylaid by the very pleasant, very beautiful, Miss Jane Penhaligon. She stopped, pleased to speak to her, and looked over just in time to catch Captain Boscowan's eyes. Even though her conversation with Eliza had been inaudible to the rest of the room, Clarissa could see in his eyes that he knew exactly what had passed between them. He smiled at her and narrowed those eyes of his just a little, an almost imperceptible nod telling her that he was on her side. What a strange thing, for she had only just met him, but she had the greatest sense that Captain Boscowan was a man who could be trusted. When his eyes flicked briefly to Daniel Morgan and then back to her, she realised that he had taken in every part of her circumstances. It afforded her an uncustomary sensation of relief, and she would not easily forget Captain Boscowan.

Chapter Fifteen

The following morning, Clarissa rose early, keen not to encounter the surly and disagreeable Lady Northcott. She had scowled at her for the remainder of the evening, likely leaving her guests in little doubt that Miss Clarissa Tate was in trouble.

Well, she could be as scornful as she wished, Clarissa would not be made to feel awkward and obliged any longer. With the prospect of rooms, possibly in Fowey, looking ever more likely, Clarissa began to feel a sense of calm, of having already overcome her enemies without them even realising it.

Nonetheless, her new calm notwithstanding, Clarissa was in no mood to deal with Eliza that morning. The large bruise on the soft skin of her upper arm had made her angry, and she had sensed that her anger might well make her a little reckless. She was most certainly changing, and she wondered if it had anything to do with Felix. Perhaps witnessing his freedom from the world had given her ideas about her own. She was *untethered*, after all.

When she sat down to breakfast, the staff were only just beginning to bring out the warm platters. The footman looked a little dismayed to see her there so early, but she declared she would just help herself to a little of whatever was ready and be very glad to have it. He smiled at her; he was growing used to her ways and that sense of easiness that he likely never felt with his employer.

After a hasty meal of eggs, toasted bread, and some hot tomatoes, all washed down with some strong coffee, Clarissa was ready to face the day. She took a slice of pound cake and wrapped it in a handkerchief, clutching it in her hand and determining to take it with her to enjoy on a morning walk.

A walk was the very best thing that she could do in her current mood, and so she fastened a very light cloak about her shoulders and strode out of the house, pleased that she had not encountered either Philip or Eliza along the way.

It was only eight o'clock and the air was still a little cool, although the sun was bright, and she knew the day would be warm. She walked across the dewy lawn and headed directly for the nearest patch of woodland. It was the thing she liked best about Northcott; it was surrounded on all sides by woodland, all the way to the edge of the estate. In amongst that woodland were various workers' and gamekeepers' cottages, even one or two of them housing retired servants. It was a kindness of the last Earl, and one she doubted would continue under the new regime.

She was wandering past just such a cottage when a movement from the little garden surrounding it caught her eye. Clarissa peered over, sheer curiosity driving her, and found herself startled when a woman with pure white hair pulled into a tight bun at the back of her head was staring right back at her.

"Hello, little miss," the woman said, walking with quick little steps to the low-cut hedge.

"Hello, Mrs...?" Clarissa began tentatively.

"Bates. I am Miss Lucy Bates," the woman said and began to laugh.

There was a vagueness to her expression, a tendency to focus on Clarissa's face and then away into the distance that was a little unsettling. The woman's attention was caught by the pound cake wrapped in the handkerchief and she stared at it without speaking for some moments.

"I am Clarissa Tate, Miss Bates," Clarissa said, trying to gain the woman's attention.

"What's in that handkerchief, little miss?" she said, addressing Clarissa in a way which suggested she had not taken in her name at all.

"It is a little slice of pound cake, Miss Bates," Clarissa said, beginning to feel waves of sympathy for the woman she was certain was not quite in full charge of her own senses.

"Ooh, I do like pound cake, little miss. Tedn't my favourite cake, but I like it all the same," she said and looked at Clarissa hopefully, almost like a child might.

"Would you like it?" Clarissa said, thinking that she would willingly forgo the treat.

"You can come into the garden if you like. I can't go out of the garden, little miss; tedn't allowed. Come in, come in. There is a little gate," Lucy Bates looked suddenly mischievous and Clarissa did not like to turn her down.

She took a few steps, opened the little wooden gate, and walked tentatively into the garden. She could not help but wonder who lived there also, for surely Lucy Bates could not be alone, not with such a fragile mind.

"Here, you take the pound cake," Clarissa said, opening the handkerchief and holding out her hand.

"Little miss, 'tis a pretty little handkerchief you have. I used to embroider the handkerchiefs for the boys."

"Your boys?" Clarissa said.

"I look after all the little ones, I do. I nurses 'em; that's my job."

"It sounds like a very fine job, Mrs Bates. You must like it very much," Clarissa decided to join her, to be a part of a conversation that was likely not based in reality; to do otherwise struck her as a little cruel.

Lucy Bates took the cake and began to eat it slowly. She closed her small dark eyes, seeming to savour every bite. Clarissa simply stood there, feeling a little awkward, but determined not to abandon her new acquaintance so soon.

Despite her white hair, Clarissa could see that Lucy was not as old as she had first imagined. In truth, she was likely in her middle to late fifties and she was reminded of the white-haired and very vital Captain Boscowan.

The prematurely snow-white hair was where their similarities ended, however. Lucy Bates was a soft looking woman; a little rotund with small, trusting eyes, wearing a plain and thick blue gown and a knitted shawl of the same colour over her shoulders.

"Lucy! Lucy! Where are you?" The voice of another woman, a much less pleasant-sounding woman, assaulted Clarissa's ears.

"I be over here, Marjorie," Lucy said through a mouthful of pound cake.

For a moment, Clarissa considered running away. She felt suddenly as if she ought not to be there, but she was rooted to the spot, perversely determined to see the owner of the strident voice. She did not have long to wait, for a very austere -looking woman with harshly curled hair the colour of steel was marching around the side of the cottage towards them. When she saw Clarissa, she almost broke her stride, but kept her eyes to fixed her as she bore down upon them.

"Forgive me, I was just speaking to Miss Bates over the hedge there, and we were sharing a little piece of pound cake," Clarissa said, feeling like a child explaining naughty behaviour to her governess.

"Well, I daresay that was very kind of you, Miss…?" she said, her cold eyes narrowing.

"Miss Tate. Clarissa Tate," Clarissa said and inclined her head politely.

"Oh, from the hall," she said, and it was clear that the woman had, at least, heard of her.

"Yes, that is right." Clarissa noted that no introduction was forthcoming from the woman Lucy had called Marjorie.

And Marjorie, whoever she was, was austerity itself in a gown that was almost aggressively black, as if she had been in mourning for her entire life. The gown was old-fashioned and high-necked, severe in every way, and her entire appearance almost made Clarissa shiver.

"Well, we shall not keep you, Miss," Marjorie attempted a smile and Clarissa rather wished she had not, for it was a forced and rather garish affair. "Dear Lucy has not been very well of late, and I must get her back inside," she went on, and her attempt at a softening of tone was even more unsettling.

"Of course, of course," Clarissa said, wanting to run but wanting to stay also; she wondered if Lucy was going to be all right with that woman. "Good day to you both. And it was nice to meet you, Miss Bates," Clarissa went on before turning to make her way back out of the garden, closing the gate behind her.

As she began to walk away, Clarissa could hear Marjorie's voice drifting across the cool morning air. There was a tone to it which made her stop in her tracks and turn to look, and she could see that Marjorie was walking Lucy away, holding her roughly by the arm, just as Eliza had done to her the night before.

Something about it made her blood boil and she hurried back, walking around the thick, blood-red rhododendron bushes; high, thick and perfect cover. She walked down the side of the cottage, unseen by the two ladies in the garden.

"You really must be careful, Lucy," Marjorie sounded exasperated. "You must remember that you have to be careful. Do you remember it, Lucy?"

"I must be careful. I must not let it slip or I will lose my place," Lucy said, like a child reciting a piece of text by rote; the mechanical response made Clarissa really shiver this time.

She pushed herself a little deeper into the rhododendrons, caring little for how it was disarranging her bonnet-less hair.

"Really, it is bad enough that *that ruffian* barges his way in here whenever he feels like it. The old Earl should have put a stop to that years ago. It will end in trouble, mark my words. Lucy, you must keep a hold of that wriggling tongue of yours," Marjorie concluded, her voice becoming nothing more than a faint hum now that the two ladies were clearly heading into the cottage.

"What are you doing?" The voice behind her was so stern and so unexpected that Clarissa gasped.

"Oh… I…" she said, her heart pounding violently. *"Felix?"* she said in surprise, hardly believing that the owner of such an angry sounding voice could be her friend.

"Yes, *Felix*," he said, narrowing his eyes. "Why are you hiding in the rhododendrons? Have you seen something of interest?" He seemed suspicious, and Clarissa found it a little upsetting.

"I was speaking to the sweet lady who lives here, a lady called Lucy. I had not sought to intrude, Felix," she said, her own voice sharpening in annoyance. "I had not sought to pry either. The fact of the matter is that it was Lucy who called me over and she was so sweet and so intent upon eating the piece of pound cake I had wrapped in a handkerchief that I did not like to deny her."

"I see," he said, his features beginning to soften.

"She seemed a little vulnerable, but very pleasant, and I must admit that when her companion arrived, I was somewhat unsettled. So yes, you find me hiding in the rhododendrons, Felix, and indeed you *do* find me *eavesdropping*. I daresay that you now believe that I have an extraordinarily prying nature, especially after the diaries, but I assure you I do not. There was something about the other woman, *Marjorie* I believe her name is, that I did not like. There was something in her tone I found unsettling, and I suffered the strongest suspicion that she is not at all kind to Lucy. So, there you have it!" By the time she had finished, Clarissa was the angry one and Felix perfectly calm.

"Forgive me, I am a little protective of Lucy Bates," he said and looked chagrined. "I spoke before I thought, Clarissa."

"Perhaps you did," Clarissa said, not ready to forgive him entirely, but not wanting to make an enemy of him either. "You are obviously fond of the sweet old thing."

"Come, let us walk away from here," he said, leading her away from the rhododendrons and into the woodland until they reached the path which would take him back in the direction of Farwynnen House.

"I assume your brother does not know you freely wander his grounds," Clarissa said, trying to add a little humour to dissolve the awkwardness between them that she still did not understand.

"Good Lord, no!" he said and laughed. "He would set the dogs upon me."

"He does not have any dogs," Clarissa said and smiled in response to his sheepish grin.

"Lucy Bates, *Miss* Lucy Bates, for she was never married, is a very dear woman, but if you spent any length of time with her, I assume you realised that she does not have full command of her mental faculties," he said, walking slowly along as if in no hurry to leave her.

"Yes, she is a little confused," Clarissa agreed. "But not alarmingly so."

"She has not always been so, for Lucy Bates was once my nurse. She had been Philip's nurse first and was still employed at Northcott when I was born."

"No wonder you are so fond of her," Clarissa said, beginning to understand his instinct to protect her.

"She suffered an illness some years ago. It was a stroke or something similar, teamed with an infection, although I do not know all the details. I know that she was terribly ill and that her mental reason suffered permanently as a consequence. My father installed her here on the estate, not wanting to turn her out or have her carted away to some awful county asylum. She is too sweet and too precious to be placed in such conditions."

"Yes, she most certainly is. Most people are," Clarissa said, and he looked at her quizzically as he had done before, as if surprised by her.

"Yes, I believe the very same. But Lucy's condition is not widely known, for my father was keen for her to be protected for the rest of her life. I do not even think that Philip is aware of it, for he was never kind to his nurse and has probably never set eyes on her since she fell ill."

"And when did she fall ill?"

"I was just a boy of ten, perhaps. Philip was a little older, as you know. He was fourteen."

"Was he not away at school? And did you not have a *tutor* by then, Felix? Or did Lucy's job at the hall change into something else?"

"She did remain at the hall and it never occurred to me that there was anything unusual in it. Lucy did not become our governess because she was a local woman of very little education, but she was not dismissed. I have never known why, but I have always been glad. She is safe here, at least as long as Philip does not turn his attention to her. I come here often because I am afraid that he will finally pay a little closer attention to his tenants and discover that she is so mentally frail. If it occurred to him to do so, he would have her committed."

"Oh no," Clarissa said, instinctively laying the flat of her palm across her heart. "You must see that I would never, ever tell him." The reason for his initial aggression towards her was finally very clear.

"Forgive me again, Clarissa. It was a reaction, a foolish instinct. In my defence, I had not realised it was you at first, for all I could see was a woman pressed hard against the rhododendrons. I really am sorry."

"Very well," Clarissa said, trying to let her fleeting sensibilities waft through her, *right through*, rather than letting them take up residence. "But who is Marjorie?"

"Ah, Marjorie Ames. She was a maid at Northcott for many years, since before I was born, certainly. I never liked her; she was a watchful and sneaky woman, and I am certain that she took many tales to my father's ears. I daresay some men are encouraged, even flattered, by what looks like unbending loyalty. I, on the other hand, trust her as much as I would a poisonous snake. Anyway, she has lived there in that cottage with Lucy for years. My father made an allowance for them both, ensuring that they would stay in that cottage for the rest of their lives."

"I cannot help but wish that your father had picked somebody who was, perhaps, kinder."

"As do I, Clarissa. That is why I call upon Lucy at least once every week. Not just to see Lucy, you understand, but to let Marjorie Ames know that I will never be far away," he said and gave a brittle smile.

"Ah, then *you* must be the *ruffian!*" Clarissa said and began to laugh.

"The ruffian?" His smiled had loosened, relaxed, and had become something more distractingly handsome; that alone was enough for Clarissa to silently forgive him.

"I heard Marjorie telling Lucy that the old Earl ought to have put a stop to the *ruffian* barging his way in."

"And you thought of me?" His heavy brows were raised high, his dark eyes finally amused.

"Not immediately, but the thing rather falls into place now."

"Does it indeed?" he tried to look scandalised.

"Yes, it does." Clarissa was relieved for the return to ease but wondered if she would ever truly know this man.

"Well, the edge of the estate beckons me, and I must leave you before I am tackled by one of the more loyal gamekeepers as a poacher or something similar," he said and laughed. "You will come to Farwynnen when you are passing, will you not? If you have not been put off by my rough manners?"

"Of course, I shall," Clarissa said, and felt a swirling of movement in her chest; the old excitement returning.

Chapter Sixteen

Feeling exhausted but not able to stop reading, Clarissa turned yet another page. She knew she had stayed awake too long, that she would feel terrible in the morning, but still she continued.

Her disappointment in scouring three more diaries and finding nothing of note had sent her back into the attics to find more. Discovering two in the bottom of yet another well-packed wooden trunk, she had managed to read the first one from cover to cover in that one sitting, propped up in bed, the hours rolling on. It was now almost three o'clock in the morning and Clarissa had been about to give in when an entry caught her eye. This was an older diary than the one she had read to Felix from, and many of the people mentioned in it thus far were people she had never heard of. But when she saw a name she recognised, the hair on the back of her neck stood up.

"12th December 1797,

Another awful day; will it never end? I have been out to the cottage and Marjorie tells me that there has been no improvement in Lucy's mental state. Old Doctor Carlyon has said that the physical effects of the stroke and complicated infections have passed, and he can see no reason at all for Lucy's confused ramblings. At first, I had thought it must surely be the infections, poisons in the body affecting the mind. A stroke does not ordinarily lead to such confusion, so Carlyon tells me, and it is only today that I have reached the conclusion which ought to have struck me as true from the very first; that I have caused the mental breakdown of Lucy Bates.

If I live to be a hundred years old, there will not be enough time in my life to repent for all I have done. And yet still I cannot find it within me to tell the truth. Perhaps Lucy's mental infirmity is a divine intervention, one designed to have my secret exposed whether I intend it or not. Still, if Lucy had said anything of sense about it, if she had admitted it at all to Marjorie Ames, there is no doubt in my mind that Marjorie would have told me already. She is a most loyal servant and one who has served me well over the years. But do I really deserve loyalty? Do I deserve to have a loyal gatekeeper, keeping the world away from whatever Lucy Bates might unwittingly say? I know I do not, and yet I fear it. Just one sentence from Lucy will be enough to peel back the layers of my deceit and reveal my dreadful burden to the world.

My life has become something almost unliveable. My secret is a burden, the twist and turns I have made to keep it gnaw at my soul. The lives of two wives utterly destroyed, even though the second of them still lives. What is a man to do? If I own up to my secret now, lives will be ruined. If I do not own up to my secret now, other lives will be ruined. There is nothing now I can do to spare the pain, for whichever way I turn, I shall be hurting somebody. Everyday I wake and I cannot believe that I am still here, that I am allowed to live with what I have done. But perhaps that is my punishment. Perhaps I really will live until I am a hundred years old just so that I might suffer every day of it. It is what I deserve, after all."

Clarissa began to flick through the pages of the diary, scanning the words for any sign of Lucy's name. Could it be right that that sweet, confused, snow-haired woman held the old Earl's secret somewhere inside, locked away in a part of her mind that she either could not access or could not convey?

Clarissa sighed with exasperation. She had found something, and yet it had not made anything clearer. If anything, adding Lucy Bates for consideration had made things more complicated. And Clarissa was simply reading through diaries, skipping backwards in time one moment, coming closer to the present in the next, depending upon which volumes she found in the attics at any given time. She needed a plan, a system, a methodical approach.

Clarissa closed the diary and tucked it under her pillow; she would hide it under the floorboards in the morning. She blew out her candle and settled down, pulling the sheets and blankets up around her neck and staring blindly into the darkness.

Thinking of Felix and his mother led her thoughts to the Earl's first wife, Jennifer. Philip's mother. If the Earl had ideas that he'd had something to atone for, some wrong he had done Jennifer, then perhaps his great secret would not be found unless she went back. Clarissa sat up in bed, although she wasn't quite sure how that was going to help. That was it! She needed to find diaries which went back to a time when Jennifer Ravenswood still lived. What had Felix said? She had died when Philip was an infant, not yet one year. So, that was in 1784. Diaries prior and up to that year must be her priority now. Any she stumbled across after that date, she would leave where they were and she would come back to them later. But if she was ever going to get the truth, Clarissa was going to have to go back in time.

Now that she had a plan, now that she felt a little method and order in it all, Clarissa laid back down, determined to sleep at last. She would get four or five hours sleep at best and she knew she did not function well when she was so deprived.

Clarissa closed her eyes and felt herself beginning to drift. When she heard a sound from outside, something so faint that it was quite miraculous it had permeated her fading consciousness, she sat bolt upright in bed once again.

Clarissa slept with her bedroom window open all year round, even if it was just a gap of an inch in the winter. She could not bear to be without fresh air, and on a summer's night, the sash window was slid almost to the top. The sound of hooting owls and screeching prey were so familiar that they did not register anymore. The sound of a footstep on the gravel beneath her window, however, could not have registered more clearly.

With her eyes adjusted to the gloom, Clarissa crossed the room by the light of the moon and peered cautiously out of the window. There was nobody below and no sound to be heard. She would have got back into bed had it not startled her. It was so quiet, so indistinct, that if Clarissa had been asleep as she ought to have been by three o'clock in the morning, she would not have been any the wiser. It was too early for the servants to be up, and too late for any visitor of good faith to be approaching the house.

With a pounding heart, she crept to the door of her chamber. Opening it just a crack, Clarissa listened intently. The silence in Northcott Hall had an almost physical quality. It felt thick, almost oppressive, the sort of silence that could panic a person and have them believe they had gone deaf.

And then she heard it; the murmur of voices from below. Her heart really was pounding now and a cold, uncomfortable perspiration had broken out around her neck and collarbone. Clarissa was afraid.

She wondered what she ought to do next and considered creeping upstairs and waking Philip and Eliza. If there were intruders in the house, what else could she do?

The idea of facing the two of them in the middle of the night and being wrong was enough to stop Clarissa doing that and, instead, she crept to the top of the stairs in near darkness and peered down. She could see nothing, no movement anywhere, but the murmur of voices returned. It was so quiet that she realised they were not standing in the entrance hall below her, but elsewhere. She felt sick and terrified. Finally, a little movement suggested that whoever was down there was now in one of the corridors which ran from the entrance hall.

"I have a place ready for you below-stairs. It is away from the servants' quarters, but we must be quiet," Clarissa's eyes flew wide open and her mouth dropped; the voice she could hear was that of Philip Ravenswood.

However quietly he spoke, he had the sort of voice which drifted. It was clear, it carried, and she was certain that, had anybody else spoken those words, she would not have heard them so distinctly. Clarissa crept down three or four steps, peering through the stair rails but seeing nothing. Everything was silence now, and she knew that Philip and whomever was with him had crept silently down one of the servants' staircases and into the lowest part of Northcott Hall.

Feeling a little emboldened by the fact that there were not intruders in the house as such, Clarissa crept further down the stairs, listening intently. There were no more voices to be heard, no footsteps, but as she turned to make her way back upstairs, she heard the faintest squeak in the distance. She stopped, frowned, and tried to imagine what the sound might have been. And then it came to her; it sounded like a hinge somewhere that needed oiling. Perhaps a door somewhere below stairs had been opened.

With nothing more she could do, Clarissa returned to her chamber. She knew now that she would be awake for some time, running it all over in her mind. Perhaps it was a servant Philip had been talking to, but who had been outside? Clarissa knew she had not dreamed that sound, she had heard it; a footstep on the gravel.

But what did it all mean? A footstep in the gravel and the squeak of an un-oiled hinge.

Chapter Seventeen

It was another fine summer's morning when Felix strode out of Farwynnen House and took the steep slope up to the coastal path at a run. He could always run up the path that even the horses struggled with, ever since he was a child visiting his beloved grandparents. Farwynnen House had been a playground to him, and Farwynnen Cove a source of endless excitement and flights of fancy.

When he reached the top of the slope, almost bursting out onto the coastal path above, a flash of red coats in the distance, further south, made him chuckle. *Soldiers.*

He watched them for a moment with some amusement, hardly able to imagine that there was much smuggling to be done by daylight. Felix knew, of course, that smuggling had never really gone away in Cornwall. What he had realised, however, that it was now back with some determination in their own little part of the world, their own slice of the Cornish coast.

As a child, Felix had loved to hear tales of smuggling from his grandfather. Whilst Jago Roscarrock had never outright told him that he had been involved in it all, he had managed to leave his grandson in no doubt whatsoever that he had. Felix thought it wonderful; exciting. What he had not realised at the time, being such a young boy, was that his grandfather very likely still allowed the odd small wooden gig to row into Farwynnen Cove, *Smugglers' Cove* as it would be forever known, to bring ashore a little contraband.

Despite the rumours which circulated, largely at his own brother's instigation, Felix was a moral and law-abiding man. But he identified with the smugglers of the last century, feeling, as many did, that the duties imposed back then on such simple things as salt and tea and brandy, for no better reason than to fund wars, had been the most immoral thing of all. Cornwall have done what she needed to do to survive; she had kept her hard-working men and women alive by providing them with a wonderfully complicated coastline and the sort of human spirit that could overcome anything.

Felix did not, however, identify in any way with the smugglers of the current day. The duties on essential imported goods had been finally lessened, mining of copper, tin, and clay in the county had become more lucrative with the advances in methods, and life had become liveable, even though it was still not easy for so many. But the poor were not at the helm anymore; smuggling was done by violent, brutish men at the behest of paymasters who sat in fine drawing rooms and lined their pockets without risk. What had once been a community acting in unison for their own survival had become yet another way for men who called themselves gentlemen to have men who needed money risk their lives.

These days, Felix wished the soldiers well in a way he might not have done as an excited boy on his grandfather's knee.

Turning his attention away from the red-clad soldiers as they stared out to sea, unaware that they were being observed by the grandson of one of the Farwynnen Cove smugglers of old, he set off across the peninsula. He was going to see Lucy and wanted to make haste. He would be off the Northcott estate before his brother had even finished his breakfast.

The cottage Lucy and Marjorie stayed in was mercifully close to the boundary line, meaning he never had to go too far into the estate to see her. He never encountered anybody there and he hoped to keep it that way. He was certain that Lucy Bates was so far beneath Philip's notice that he would have quite forgotten that she even existed. If he ever discovered that Felix still visited her after all these years, he would certainly find a way to put a stop to it. If that happened, Lucy Bates would be all alone. All alone with Marjorie Ames.

When he reached the cottage, he wasted no time in striding up the path and knocking loudly on the door. Marjorie Ames opened it almost immediately, as if she had seen him approaching from within, and scowled at him as she did every time they met.

"It is not convenient today, sir," she began, attempting a pleasant tone and failing miserably. "I am afraid Lucy is not well and she is in bed," she went on.

"Then I will see her there," Felix said and walked past her, already heading for the stairs with Marjorie in pursuit.

"That is not proper, sir. That is not right," Marjorie objected as she darted up the stairs behind him.

"What is not proper, Miss Ames, is a lack of kindness and caring for a woman who is sweet and vulnerable. She cared for me when I was a child, and I will never be dissuaded from returning that kindness. Now, if you will excuse me," he said and gave her a brittle smile before opening the door to Lucy's room, stepping inside, and closing it in Marjorie's face.

Lucy was indeed in bed but sitting up looking fit and healthy as she ate her breakfast from a tray. She smiled at him happily as he crossed the room to sit down on the very edge of her bed.

"Hello, Lucy," he said, feeling his heart open and warm as it always was when he saw his old nurse.

Lucy Bates had been such a loving influence in his early life, somehow managing to soothe the confusion of his mother's despair and his father's indifference. But it was his father's indifference to his mother, not to Felix. If Felix was honest, his father had doted on him. It was not until he was a little older that he had become uncomfortable with the situation and no longer glowed under the Earl's unstinting attention. If he could show such love to a child, how could he not show it to his wife? That was when the confusion and the need to know had begun to set in. Felix was still a small boy, unable to put his own fear and upset into words, but Lucy had just seemed to know; she had soothed him and, more often than not, she had made the world right for him, even if it was always only a temporary solution.

"Oh, you are a fine man now," Lucy said, her eyes focused in a way that they were not always. "Such a handsome man and so tall. That hair of yours needs a little attention though, Arnold. I never thought to see you with such unruly hair. 'Tis a shame, Arnold, because it covers that lovely face of yours. But I would say that, wouldn't I? Tedn't right though, to be covering a face so fine." She was still smiling, quickly returning her attention to the breakfast on her lap.

"You always say the kindest things to me, Lucy. Wherever would I be in this world without your praise? Nowhere, that is where," he said and laughed.

Lucy laughed also, but he knew it was not his words she laughed at; she simply laughed because he laughed, like a child trying to please an adult. It both warmed him and broke his heart at the same time, as almost every visit to that little cottage could do.

"I saw a *little miss*, you know," Lucy said, waving a small piece of toasted bread this way and that as she embarked upon a tale. "I used to embroider handkerchiefs for the boys. I liked *her* handkerchief; I wanted to keep it, but I didn't dare ask."

"Yes, I remember the embroidered handkerchiefs, Lucy," Felix said, seizing upon the only part of her confusing little story he understood.

"I never did sew an A onto them though. I wish I had now, for it would have been fitting." She dropped the toasted bread onto her plate uneaten.

"Come on, Lucy, you have to eat something, or you will be hungry all day long," Felix cajoled kindly, reaching out to pick up the toasted bread and push it gently into her hands.

Felix had stayed with her until she had eaten all her breakfast, rising only when her eyes began to close, and her head began to nod. He made his way quietly out of the room with the intention of finding Marjorie and asking her to make Lucy more comfortable in the bed so that she could go back to sleep but found he did not have to look too far for her. Marjorie Ames was standing on the other side of the door, surprised when it opened. So, old habits never died; she was still a sneaky little woman.

"Lucy is asleep, so could you make her more comfortable?" Felix said, glaring at her.

"Yes, of course," she said and made to move around him.

"Who is Arnold?" Felix said, barring her way.

"I have no idea."

"She called me Arnold today, as I am sure you will have overheard," he said, ignoring her bristling offence. "But it is not the first time she has called me Arnold and I wonder who it is she confuses me with. You have lived with her all these years in this cottage and you knew her up at the hall, how can it be that you have no idea?"

"You know how confused she is, sir. Arnold might be somebody from her childhood or somebody who never existed in the first place and I think it is a little rich of you to say such a thing. You always upset her, and I wish you would not come," she finished with a snarl.

"Upset her? I have made sure she has eaten every bit of her breakfast and she is now asleep. I would say that she is calm, not upset."

"She came from one of those sprawling families in Telland, the sort of family which burdens itself with endless children," Marjorie began, the disdain that one working class person could have for another never failing to amaze him. "There will have been brothers and sisters all over the place, I'll be bound; perhaps Arnold was a little brother, one she now thinks is you. I am afraid that is the best I can do, for it is always a guess as far as Lucy is concerned. The bigger chance is that she made it up altogether. She's always making things up".

"I will be back next week," Felix said, finally turning away from her, unable to bear her company for a moment longer.

Felix walked down the stairs, through the cottage, and out into the warm Summer's day, wishing there was something he could do to release Lucy Bates from a lifetime of the company of Marjorie Ames.

Chapter Eighteen

"Where are you going, Clarissa?" Eliza said, the heels of her flat dress-boots clicking noisily across the tiled floor of the entrance hall, giving Clarissa the strange impression that she was being chased.

"I have an engagement this afternoon, Lady Northcott." Clarissa turned slowly and held Eliza's gaze.

Ever since Eliza had bruised her arm, Clarissa had barely been able to contain her contempt for her. No longer did she creep about Northcott in the way she had done for the last three years. She was not afraid anymore; she was not a child but a grown woman who had options. Limited options, granted, but options she was grateful for. This would only persist for as long as she stayed and allowed it.

"No, no, no, no!" Eliza said, losing her temper like a child.

"Lady Northcott?" Clarissa said, her voice calm and her eyebrows raised in what she hoped Eliza would recognise as condescension.

"Daniel Morgan is coming to tea this afternoon, and I expect you to form a part of our little party."

"Perhaps if you had mentioned it before, Lady Northcott," Clarissa began, seeing Eliza's fury ignited in her eyes. "But I am afraid that I am already engaged and am expected to take tea with Lord and Lady Marchmont this afternoon. If I do not leave shortly, I shall be late." The truth was that she had very rarely taken tea with Lord Marchmont present, but she thought mentioning his name too would do something to lessen Eliza's annoyance. She was, of course, wrong.

"Oh, that foul woman!" Eliza said, losing control of herself in a way a countess ought never to do, even in private.

"I understand you do not like her, that is your right. But I like Lady Marchmont very much and it is for me to choose my friends, not you. I have no interest in Daniel Morgan; not now, not ever. I cannot have you believe you have a right over my life, a right to make choices about who I will and will not see, for you do not." And with that, Clarissa turned and began to stride towards the door.

Eliza chased her, reaching out to grab her arm, but Clarissa immediately and strongly shook herself free. Eliza looked furious, her cheeks red and her eyes blazing.

"You will stay!" she said, just a hair's breadth away from shouting.

"I will not!" Clarissa said quietly but fiercely. "And do not *ever* lay a hand upon me again."

"Who do you think you are? A simple Baronet's daughter and nothing more. No title, no fortune! I am the Countess of Northcott!"

"Then perhaps you might consider behaving as such, *My Lady*," Clarissa's voice dripped so much sarcasm that she could hardly believe it herself.

Just months ago, she would have been made afraid by this, but not now. She was *untethered*. The very word in her mind made her think of Felix and she couldn't help but smile.

"Do not smirk at me!" Eliza's voice was raw now.

"I am smiling, not smirking. And I am also leaving now," Clarissa turned away from her.

"We do not have to keep you here, Clarissa Tate!"

"No, of course you do not." Clarissa said calmly; the moment was coming, and she knew it was.

"I am going to speak to Philip, and he will demand that you stay here at Northcott today."

"I will not."

"Then I cannot see it is possible for you to continue to live here. What you say to that? What do you say to Philip casting you out for the inconvenience that you are? You were never welcome here, Clarissa. You were never anything more than a physical manifestation of my father-in-law's ridiculous sentimentality."

"I do not think I have ever been so thoroughly described," Clarissa said and laughed. "Of course, it is right that I should go, and I shall. Have no fear, Lady Northcott, I shall speak to my father's attorney, Mr Godolphin, tomorrow. He administers my annuity and, if I tell him of the great urgency of the situation, I am sure he will have secured me some very suitable rooms in no time at all. I will not inconvenience you any further and I am truly sorry if I ever have," Clarissa was smiling, her spirits soaring into the sky.

She had never been so utterly reckless and so absolutely in control at the same time. This was *her* life, and she would not have it dictated to her, not when she had been given the wonderful gift of emancipation. As Felix had advised her, it was not a thing to be wasted. She did not care if she had no more than two rooms in Fowey, she was free, and she always would be. She did not care if she ever sat down to eat with lords and ladies again; freedom was a far greater privilege.

Eliza was open-mouthed, her lips working as if she was about to speak, but no sound came. Clarissa could not escape the idea that the dreadful woman was somehow regretting her hasty words and wild temper. But why should she? It did not make sense.

Clarissa finally made her way outside, walking smartly to the stable block and asking for her horse to be saddled. She would be pleased to be in Gwendolyn Marchmont's company; what an irony that a woman such as Eliza Ravenswood could ever dare to describe that fine lady as *foul*.

As one of the stable lads led her saddled horse out to her, Clarissa became aware of running footsteps approaching. She turned quickly, surprised not to see Eliza flying towards her, but Philip.

"Clarissa, my dear," he said, breathlessly and full of disingenuous care.

"Lord Northcott?" Clarissa said, relishing the feeling of unexpected calm.

"You must forgive Eliza, my dear, she is a little out of sorts at the moment. Truly, I think she is about to fall ill, although I will not worry you with the details. But I can assure you that she did not mean what she said, not for a minute. Of course, you are not a burden to us, and of course you must stay."

Clarissa looked at him quizzically; she could hardly believe what she was hearing, and his words, not to mention his rather desperate demeanour, unsettled her. When had he decided that Clarissa Tate was a valuable addition to the household? None of it rang true.

"Still, since I no longer have a guardian, it seems that I quite rightly do not have a place here. I do not expect more than your excellent father gave me. Lord Northcott's promise to my father was kept, and kept well, and I am truly grateful for it. But perhaps it is right now that I should go," she said, if only to see what reaction he would have to it.

"Oh please, I would not want you to go, Clarissa. You are a part of the family now, my dear, and Eliza and I would miss you greatly. The servants adore you, and Northcott would never be the same again. Please, Clarissa, you must not think of leaving, really you must not." And with that he took her hands in his own and gave them a squeeze.

If she had been concerned before, she was entirely discombobulated now. Philip had never made any display of such pleasure in her presence, rather he had only ever either ignored her or eyed her with disdain. This behaviour gave her a most uncomfortable sensation, and she could not wait to be away from him and hear Lady Marchmont's forthright views on the matter.

"Well, how very kind of you," Clarissa said and smiled.

"You will not speak to Mr Godolphin just yet, will you? Just give it a little time. For me," he added the last with a boyish, beseeching look.

"Of course, Lord Northcott," she said, knowing that she truly had no intention of staying at Northcott Hall forever, but wanting to placate him for now, to have him release her so that she might spend the afternoon in vastly better company.

Clarissa had never been so relieved to ride into St Austell as she was on that day. She was more relieved still when she arrived in Lady Marchmont's townhouse drawing room to find her sitting with none other than Felix Ravenswood.

"Ah, my dear Clarissa," Lady Marchmont said, rising to greet her warmly, holding her hands and kissing her cheek. "Naturally I invited Felix. You do not mind, do you?"

"I think I had quite expected it, My Lady," Clarissa said humorously and both Lady Marchmont and Felix laughed.

"But tell me, why do you look so flustered?" Lady Marchmont went on, gently pushing her guest down into a seat. "If you are not surprised to see Felix here, then why do you have such high colouring?" As always, Gwendolyn Marchmont got straight to the point.

"I have had a most curious morning. I am glad to be here, it is true, for I wonder if you would not mind my relaying the circumstances to you both and having your opinions. Understand, please, that it is not in my nature to give every detail of my home life, but Lord and Lady Northcott are not my family, and so I feel a little freer to do so."

"Oh, wonderful! Hold nothing back, my dear, I do like a good bit of intrigue," Lady Marchmont said, her eyes and her smile both wide.

"Yes, do not hold anything back," Felix said, his voice a little more serious than Lady Marchmont's; perhaps even a little concerned.

Clarissa gave them every bit of conversation that she had had with both Eliza and Philip that morning in as much detail as she could remember. Lady Marchmont's expression changed with every sentence, one moment amused and scandalised, the next all admiration for her young friend's open defiance.

"Oh, what I would have given to hear you defy the countess so boldly. How delicious!"

"Delicious, perhaps, Gwendolyn, but I think a little concerning also," Felix said, less amused and excited than their hostess.

"Why, Felix?" Clarissa said, knowing that she had felt unsettled by it herself and interested to hear Felix's perception.

"It strikes me that this is all in their determination to have you married to the pasty-faced Daniel Morgan," Felix began, lightly interrupted by Lady Marchmont.

"Pasty faced, is he?" she said, refusing to let go of her amusement even in the face of Felix's seriousness.

"He is a little," Clarissa's little aside was designed to indulge her friend, and it worked wonderfully; Lady Marchmont chuckled with delight.

"We have to wonder at the reasons for such behaviour, do we not? What is there to be gained in my brother having you married to somebody very specific? He has no rights over you, and therefore could expect no dowry to be paid. Even if he did, there is no need for such money to be paid into the Northcott coffers, for they are already full to bursting. So, what else is there?"

"Perhaps he just wants to have rid of her?" Lady Marchmont said and then turned to Clarissa. "I do apologise, my dear, but it is a possibility."

"Not at all, Lady Marchmont, I have never been assured of my place at Northcott." Clarissa smiled at her.

"But it is *not* a possibility, is it? Gwendolyn, do concentrate," Felix said a little roughly.

"Very well, enlighten us!" Lady Marchmont fought back, but with great humour.

"The idea that the reason for having Clarissa married to be rid of her does not work. If that was the case, they would simply cast her out; they need not marry her away to achieve it. Philip is not her guardian, and as such he has no responsibility for her. And was it not Philip himself who, in this exciting tale, chased Clarissa to the stables to beg her to stay? Hand-holding, pleading expression and all!" he finished, and both Clarissa and Lady Marchmont nodded thoughtfully.

"Something is not right, is it?" Finally, Lady Marchmont was serious; so serious that Clarissa felt a little flash of fear.

"No, something is not right." Felix turned to Clarissa; those dark brooding eyes boring into her. "You must be careful, Clarissa. I do not wish to frighten you, for I honestly cannot say I understand my brother's motives. I just want you to be on your guard, to be vigilant, and to remember what I said to you on the night my father died."

"What did you say?" Lady Marchmont said, leaning forward in her seat with her eyebrows raised.

"On this one occasion, Gwendolyn, you really are going to have to mind your own business," Felix said, and Lady Marchmont roared with laughter.

"And they say *I* speak my mind!" she said. "Now then, do pull the bell-rope for tea, Felix. All this news has made me hungry."

Chapter Nineteen

When the afternoon was over, Clarissa and Felix made their way to the stables together. Clarissa was feeling unsettled by the day's events and Felix's concern. But she was also a little excited by Felix's concern, if it meant he truly cared about her.

"I know it is a long way back and you might be a little late," Felix began just before they arrived at the stables. "But if you took a rambling route, you would have to pass by Farwynnen."

"Yes, I suppose I would," Clarissa said, feeling a little excited; did he want to continue their conversation?

"And I am sure that Bess will be very pleased to see you. You made a great impression on her, you see, with your kindness."

"Oh yes, it would be lovely to see her," Clarissa said, her heart speeding up a little; she knew now he wanted her to go to the house, perhaps he had something to say to her that he could not say in front of Lady Marchmont.

"I will set off first and ride quickly; it is probably best if we are not seen together. Who knows what eyes and ears watch and listen and report back to Northcott Hall?"

"I will come directly down to the house," Clarissa confirmed and nodded.

She enjoyed the ride back from St Austell, it was a good, long stretch for her horse. Felix was not entirely out of sight, for she could just see him in the distance throughout the entirety of the journey home. She lost sight of him just at the end, imagining that he had already dropped down that steep path into Smugglers' Cove. She slowed a little, seeing the red jackets of soldiers in the distance. Were they coming towards her, or going away from her? It made a difference, for if dear Captain Boscowan was amongst the party, she did not want him to see her disappearing into Smugglers' Cove.

Clarissa finally drew her horse to a stop, watching the soldiers until she realised, with relief, that they were heading further south along the coast of the Gribben Peninsula. She let them go a little further, certain that if they turned and looked at her now, they would hardly be able to make her out at all. As soon as she was comfortable, Clarissa slid from her horse's saddle and led him down the steep path.

By the time she walked her horse around to the stable, Felix had already removed the saddle from his own.

"Put him into the stable and let us go into the house and see if Bess will bless us with more tea," he said with a smile.

"Are you in any doubt?" Clarissa said with amusement.

"She may or she may not; *tedn't a thing to be assured of, miss,*" he said, giving a startlingly accurate impression of his housekeeper.

"If she hears you, you will be in trouble," Clarissa said, stifling a laugh.

In the end, Bess Pengelly had been delighted to brew her wickedly strong tea for that charming young Miss Tate.

It was not until they were settled and alone in that wonderful, large, medieval space, comfortable in armchairs, that they began to speak seriously.

"I almost did not come, Felix, for there were soldiers on the peninsula and I thought they were coming towards me."

"Ah, you did not wish to be seen going into Smugglers' Cove?" he said. "Perhaps they would think you were a smuggler," his chuckle became a laugh.

"No, much worse than that," she said, laughing also. "I thought that Captain Boscowan might be part of the little party and, if he recognised me, might give me away at Northcott."

"Captain Boscowan?" he said and raised his eyebrows.

"His is the Captain of the Militia here in this part of Cornwall. They have been sent to patrol the coastline looking for smugglers."

"Yes, I have seen them patrolling once or twice myself. But the more of them arrive, the more I realise I will have no peace here."

"Why?"

"Clarissa, this is not known as Smugglers' Cove without good reason."

"Yes, but that must surely be historical. I am sure there has not been a smuggler here since…" she said, stopping when she saw the look on his face.

"Since my grandfather's time," he added and stared at her as if trying to gauge her reaction.

"You are not saying that…"

"That my grandfather was involved in smuggling? Yes, that is exactly what I am saying. But they were very different times and it was not done lightly; I am sure of it. When duties were high, I do believe that my grandparents were both very heavily involved in that most famous Cornish industry. And of course, nobody, you must realise, could ever smuggle a thing through this very cove without the permission or complicity of the occupant," he added, still staring at her.

"I had not given it any thought, Felix, but I am not insensible of our most recent history here. If I were to judge your grandparents, I would be judging most of Cornwall, would I not? I would be judging poor people who had to fight to survive and I most certainly would never do such a thing. And would I not probably also be judging my own father? A man who was never without tobacco or brandy even when the duties were so high that even the wealthiest balked at paying them. No, Felix, I do not judge," Clarissa said and saw his features soften.

"I should have realised, should I not?"

"With what you know of me thus far, I suppose so, yes. But why should you get no peace now? Estranged as you are from the estate, you are still the son of the old Earl of Northcott. And, as you say, nobody could smuggle contraband through here without your complicity, and who would suspect you of that?"

"Who would suspect me? A profligate man who drinks and gambles! Does the rumour not spring to mind and give you pause for thought?" he said and raised his eyebrows.

"But do you really do those things? And answer me freely, Felix, it is not an idle curiosity."

"No, I do not do those things and never have. An occasional game of cards with Sir Hugh Trevithick in Tywardreath is hardly the mark of a profligate lifestyle." As he spoke, she was reminded of the time she had seen him stumbling around outside Sir Hugh's house and knew now, more than ever, that it really had been an act. "And so occasional as to be only once or twice a year. It is hardly a propensity for gambling, is it? And alcohol? Very little. Giving you sherry the first time you came here in lieu of tea really and truly was because I had no Bess Pengelly to look after us."

"Then why do you not say it? Why do you allow half of Cornwall to believe the things your brother says about you?" she said, a little exasperated.

"Because my friends know me for who I am, Clarissa, and the opinion of everybody else does not matter."

"Unless that opinion becomes the sort of gossip that has soldiers hovering just up on the coastal path here," she said, pointing to indicate.

"Yes, I suppose this is the one downside to it. But now the thing seems to be set in stone, and it is hardly the time to start professing my firm moral fibre, is it? I would simply look as if I had something to hide," he said and laughed.

"Then I shall have to be careful in the future, not to be spied by a soldier when I come to Smugglers' Cove." Clarissa laughed.

"I think you will have to be careful wherever you go. I really did mean what I said this afternoon; do not let your guard down, Clarissa. My brother is a hateful man and I cannot say how far he might push this business of Daniel Morgan." He shook his head. "Or *why*; that is the crux of it, is not it?"

"Yes, I believe it is."

Chapter Twenty

Some days later, Clarissa felt the atmosphere to be returning to normal at Northcott. Eliza was vacantly pleasant and mildly dismissive, just as she had always been, as if no raging quarrel had ever existed between them.

Philip seemed a little embarrassed, but Clarissa could not imagine for a moment that it had anything to do with his wife's dreadful behaviour. Perhaps it had been the way he had pleaded with her to stay which had rubbed the edges off his pride. Whatever it was, Clarissa did not care.

She had not seen Felix for days, deciding to keep to the house for a while and continue to study the old Earl's diaries. She needed to make progress, to get to the bottom of this secret.

When they had finished talking of smuggling at Farwynnen House, Clarissa had told Felix of the diary entry pertaining to Lucy Bates and Marjorie Ames. They had not been able to talk over it for long, for it had been getting late and she knew she would have to return home. He had been interested, though, and seemed pleased by all her hard work. But Clarissa could not escape the fact that she had been consumed by her own little mysteries in the last few days and it was refreshing to turn her attention back to whatever secret lay at the heart of the Ravenswood family.

After another long night of scouring the old Earl's carefully written diaries, Eliza awoke feeling a little jaded. Flo Pettigrew, despite enjoying her unofficial role as Clarissa's personal maid, knocked gently and walked into the room with very rounded shoulders.

"Flo? What is it?" Clarissa said, having already dressed herself but glad that Flo was there to help her with her hair.

"It is nothing, Miss," Flo said sweetly and tried to smile; Clarissa could almost feel the poor young woman's concern.

"No, that will not do, Flo. I cannot have you looking so worried. Oh, my goodness, come closer," Clarissa stared at her. "You look as if you have not slept a wink all night!" she went on as she surveyed the heavy bags under Flo's eyes.

"Oh, Miss, I did not! Oh, I am so terribly frightened," Flo said, and Clarissa wholeheartedly believed her.

"Come, sit down on the stool," Clarissa said, leading her across the room and gently sitting her down on the velvet covered stool at the dressing table where Clarissa ordinarily sat whilst Flo saw to her hair. She rested her hands upon Flo's shoulders and could feel the poor young maid quaking just a little.

"Thank you, Miss," Flo said, sounding embarrassed as well as upset.

"Oh Flo, you must tell me everything. You know you might trust me entirely, just as I trust you. At least give me the opportunity to help you, whatever it is," Clarissa implored her.

"You might think me silly, Miss, when I tell you that I heard a noise here in the house last night," Flo said, and Clarissa felt that cold perspiration break out on her neck just as it done the night she herself had heard a noise.

"Flo Pettigrew, I will never, ever, think you silly. Now do tell me," Clarissa's bossy tone was heavily coated in care.

"Well, I woke up in the middle of the night, Miss. I'd had a strange dream of some sort, one of the type that you can hardly remember by the time your eyes are focused again, you know?"

"Yes, I know," Clarissa said encouragingly, her hands still on Flo's shoulders.

"Well, once I was awake, I came over a little thirsty. I thought to get myself a cup of milk from the kitchen, and so I crept out that way, knowing the servants would all be asleep for it was almost three o'clock in the morning," she went on, and Clarissa could feel Flo relaxing even just in the telling of it.

"Go on," she prompted.

"Well, I was in the kitchen and just about to go to the pantry to find the milk when I heard a noise somewhere outside."

"Outside of the hall?"

"No Miss, outside of the kitchen. I blew out my candle for I can always find my way around Northcott in the dark. Anyway, I crossed the kitchen to the door on the other side of it, the door leading away from the servants' quarters. I knew the sound came from there, like a footstep, and I wondered who was there. I do not know why I did it, Miss, but I went all the way to that door and I peeked around the edge."

"And?" Clarissa said, her heart almost in her mouth with fearful excitement.

"Bless me if I did not almost come face-to-face with the most frightening, ugly man I have ever seen," Flo said, her hand raising to her chest and settling over her heart. "Thank God I had thought to blow out the candle, for he would have seen me otherwise."

"You saw him? You saw him quite clearly?" Clarissa said, trying to get her bearings in this story.

"He was just a little along the corridor outside the kitchen door, Miss. He stood just where one of the barred basement windows gave a little light from the moon. Luckily for me it fell upon him and not me, otherwise I don't think I would be sitting here now telling you about it. Oh, Miss, he really was a frightening -looking man. So rough and so big, and a look about him as if he would knock you to the ground and chew the skin off your face why you lay unconscious," she said, her pretty eyes wide.

"My goodness, Flo! What a description!" Clarissa said and laughed gently, trying to soothe Flo's fractured nerves. "You will have frightened yourself half to death thinking such things."

"Oh, but if you had seen him, Miss, you would know what I meant. He looks like one of those desperate sorts of men that you imagine chained to a wall inside Dartmoor Prison."

Clarissa had the most distinct mental picture of the man, knowing that Flo's lurid imagination had most certainly added to it. But what was a man like that doing below stairs at Northcott Hall in the middle of the night?

"No wonder you are so afraid, my dear. What a terrible shock you have had," Clarissa squeezed Flo's shoulders.

"As shocking as it was, Miss, there was a bigger shock to come," Flo said, warming a little to her theme as she neared what was clearly the crescendo of this story.

"What?"

"As I stood there hardly daring to breathe or move less I be found, there came a voice from a little further away, a voice beckoning the man, I am sure, even though I could not make out what he was saying."

"Flo, did you recognise the voice?" Clarissa said, with a horrible feeling that she knew what was coming.

"Forgive me for saying it out loud, Miss, but it was His Lordship. I would know his voice anywhere, Miss, I am not making it up. He has such a voice that he cannot quite whisper, you see." Flo looked up at her as if expecting chastisement.

"Yes, you are quite right, Flo. No forgiveness is required, you are only telling the truth."

"It all went quiet after that, but I was still too frightened to move. And then there came a dreadful squeak, from somewhere further into the house, although I think it was still below stairs."

"Like a hinge that needs oiling?" Clarissa said, remembering the squeak she herself had heard in the dead of night.

"Yes, just exactly like that!" Flo said, seemingly relieved to have the noise suitably identified. "I can't stop wondering what His Lordship was doing with an awful man like that who looked as if he was so thoroughly bad."

"You must not worry about it anymore. You have told me, and you must leave it with me, do you understand?"

"You will not tell on me, will you? You will not tell His Lordship that I saw the man and I heard him?"

"Goodness me, of course not!" Clarissa smiled warmly. "Flo, I would never do anything in the world to hurt you. I would much sooner crown the new Earl of Northcott with a brass candlestick than say anything that might cause you harm," Clarissa said with such vehemence that Flo clapped a hand over her mouth to hide her giggles.

"Oh Miss, I do feel so much better, thank you." Flo suddenly looked a little tearful, as if the whole thing had been too much.

"Well I am glad of that at least," Clarissa said. "And you must keep it quiet. Stay secret about it, my dear, telling nobody but me. I do not know what to do about it yet, but I shall have a good long think about."

"Oh yes, I would not dare to tell it to anybody but you, Miss."

Eventually, Flo curled her mistress' hair into a somewhat less than perfect bun on the back of her head. Still, given the poor young woman's tortured nerves, Clarissa made no mention of it.

When she was finally alone, Clarissa continued to sit in front of the mirror, staring at herself but not really seeing. Her mind was fully occupied, for she knew that she knew something, she just did not quite know what. It was tantalisingly out of reach as she thought back over the last days and weeks. She thought of the noises she had heard herself, of how it had surprised her to hear Philip's voice drifting through the silent night. Then there was the squeak of a hinge, the very thing that Flo had heard also. She closed her eyes, concentrating hard. What had Philip said that night in the darkness?

"I have a place ready for you below-stairs. It is away from the servants' quarters, but we must be quiet." The very thought of it made her shiver now, for Clarissa thought she was finally beginning to understand.

Things were falling into place a little; not entirely, but enough to remove at least a little of the confusion which hung about Northcott Hall in so many ways.

The lateness of the hour, the footsteps, the ugly, desperate man, the squeaking hinge. She was reminded of her conversation with Captain Boscowan, how he had talked of so many smugglers' hides in Bodmin that he had never been able to find. She thought of Felix's words, how smuggling was now orchestrated by wealthy men for whom too much was never enough. And then she knew, without a doubt, that somewhere in the lower ground of Northcott Hall was a place where smuggled contraband was hidden. She did not know why, and it certainly did not make sense for Philip to do something so reckless, but she would certainly not get to the bottom of it all sitting staring at her own reflection.

She was so tired; she knew she would not cross the Peninsula to Smugglers' Cove that day. She would give herself a rest, reclining in her chamber and reading through yet another of the Earl's diaries. She would go to Felix tomorrow and she would tell him everything.

Chapter Twenty-One

It was early evening and dusky when Felix, standing at one of the arched windows and staring out into the darkening sea, saw a flash of red; movement. He immediately made his way out of the house, striding across the flag stones outside to see who had seen fit to drop down into Farwynnen Cove. He knew the red meant only one thing; a soldier.

"Can I help you?" he said, realising that the man in front of him was doing nothing to hide himself.

"You are Felix Ravenswood, are you not?" The man was smiling, walking towards him quite affably.

"I am he," Felix said, wishing he had not sounded so suspicious.

"Captain Boscowan," the man said, introducing himself and bowing his head full of thick white hair.

"Good evening, Captain. You must forgive me, I do not get many visitors here in Farwynnen Cove, and certainly not at this hour."

"Farwynnen Cove?" The Captain said, raising his eyebrows and seeming amused; Felix knew exactly what was coming next. "I forget this place has a real name and that name is not Smugglers' Cove."

"Indeed, although I daresay the name has stuck over the decades," Felix said, keen to put a little distance between himself and his maternal family's dubious past.

"Times change, sir, right enough," the Captain said, his gentle Cornish accent an asset to him, for it was curiously easy to like the man, even though he had not entirely come down onto the cove in good faith. "But sometimes, as the saying goes, the more things change, the more they stay the same." He was gently antagonising him; looking for a reaction.

"Perhaps they do and perhaps they do not. And believe me, if the fishermen of Cornwall could not afford the duty on salt to preserve the pilchard catch these days, you might well have a good reason for coming here. You will know of the old habit of this place, of how it came to be known as Smugglers' Cove, I have no doubt. As much as I have no doubt of why you are here now, Captain Boscowan. You have come here to see if the grandson shares the grandfather's sentiments."

"I like your directness, surely I do," the Captain said and laughed, gently and in a friendly way, although Felix knew that the Captain was not a man who would be easily duped. "It makes it easier for me to ask if you do, indeed, share your grandfather's sentiments."

"In my grandfather's time, I would most certainly have shared his sentiments," Felix said, somewhat defiantly. "But this is not my grandfather's time, Captain Boscowan, and I do not seek to line my pockets at the expense of others. Moreover, I do not seek to line the pockets of wealthier men than I. It is a very different thing these days; much more of a crime than ever it was before."

"It has always been a crime, sir." The Captain's amusement was clear.

"To some more than others. I am not sure starving men cared much about the consequences."

"Then they have something in common with our modern smugglers, sir. Well, I thank you for you time and bid you a good evening." The Captain inclined his head again.

"So, shall I expect more such visits to my quiet cove?"

"Oh, perhaps, sir," the Captain said with an air of affable mischief which Felix felt certain held a deeper threat beneath the surface.

"Well, good evening," Felix said and smiled as genuinely as he could, having that sense of feeling guilty even though he had done nothing to deserve it.

For the rest of the evening, Felix was left with the impression that the Captain rather liked him, but that he would not trust him as far as he could hurl him. Well, the feeling was mutual.

He had not slept well that night, a mixture of thoughts fighting for supremacy in his mind, and he awoke feeling a little surly and out of sorts.

His mood, which Bess Pengelly had commented upon more than once and at great length, was greatly improved by the unexpected arrival of Clarissa. She looked pink-cheeked and her eyes were wide and little excited. He could see she was carrying another of the little leather-bound volumes of his father's private thoughts, and his stomach began to churn.

Bess gladly made them tea and even brought in a little plate of her heavy but delicious strawberry scones. She really did like Clarissa, no doubt about it.

When the two had eaten their scones and were enjoying their second cup of tea, Clarissa held the little diary out in front of her.

"I have so much to tell you today, Felix, that I hardly know where to begin. But perhaps the most important thing I have to tell you is what I have lately discovered in yet another one of your father's diaries. Would you like to hear it? Would you like to read it for yourself?" She smiled and looked directly into his eyes, affecting him right down to his bones. "Or would you prefer not to hear it, for that is always understood?"

"Read it to me, Clarissa, just like did the first time," he said and closed eyes, leaning his head against the high-back of the armchair and waiting with anticipation; the awful anticipation of sweeping, uncontrollable emotions assailing him.

In the end, the excerpt from the diary was far more informative and far less emotional than previously.

"3rd April 1787

It has been almost four years and still I can see that my man, Carlson, carries my burden almost as much as I carry it myself. I can see it in his eyes. I have been able to see it in his eyes from the very first, but still he remains loyal to me. How many lives I have ruined with this, and how many more lives to come. As I await the birth of my second child, I find myself spiralling into a pit of despair. I allowed myself that little happiness with Morwenna, that spark of hope that I might do something better with my life, I might be a better man. But knowing that my child will soon be here, the realisation that I do not have a right to this happiness, any of it, has landed in my heart with the weight of a stone. Happiness is not mine to take. A happy life for me would be an offence to earth and heaven, I know it. A part of me wishes I could just forget, that I could greet my child, let my love for my new young wife blossom, and live as if none of this had ever happened. I was so close to doing just that, but I suppose that none of us can outrun our conscience and mine, finally, has caught up with me and is keeping step with me. I am sure it will keep step with me now and for the rest of my days. Perhaps there is a little comfort in the idea that happiness shall not be mine. A perverse comfort, an idea of penance.

Penance is precisely what should be mine, for when I looked into Carlson's eyes this morning, really looked at him for the first time in a very long time, I was reminded of just what I owe. He is a good man, but he knows where my secret is kept. He knows where my lie is buried but I know he will never tell it.

What manner of a creature am I to find I am unable to stem the tide of my own relief in knowing that Carlson would never breathe a word? I am a creature, but I shall atone in other ways. I shall deny myself that happiness, I must. Even though I know that poor Morwenna will be yet one more person to suffer by my silent need to repent."

When Clarissa had finished reading, a little silence opened, but it did not persist.

"Who is Carlson?" She said with a sort of breathy excitement as he opened his eyes and looked at her, relieved that he did not feel so waylaid by emotion as he had done before.

"Carlson was my father's valet for years and years. He was older than my father, perhaps ten or twelve years older. Anyway, as he became older and a little frailer, my father retired him to a comfortable living in a small cottage on the east of the estate, clear across Northcott from Lucy Bates."

"He still lives?" she said, her excitement telling him exactly where she was going with her conversation.

"Yes, he still lives."

"Shall we go? Shall we speak to him?"

"No, not yet, Clarissa," he said, regretful of her look of disappointment. "Without a doubt, he knows whatever secret it was that tore at my father's soul all these years. I cannot thank you enough for bringing me this far, Clarissa, for I would never have this much without you and trust me, I am most determined to continue. But Carlson was a very loyal man, he had been my father's valet since my father himself had been little more than an overgrown boy. If he has held the secret for so long, I think he might continue to hold it, even if we question him. I cannot help but think we will only have the truth from him if we have a few more facts tucked away in our sleeves. Not to mention the fact that I do not want to be found unnecessarily wandering the east side of the estate, closer to the hall itself, whilst Captain Boscowan is keeping such a firm eye on me." He saw her expression change.

"But why? Why should Captain Boscowan take such an interest in you? Even with the history of Smugglers' Cove, surely…"

"He was here last night, Clarissa. He walked down into the cove as bold as if he owned the place, not seeking to hide or creep about. He wanted me to know that he is watching me, that was the purpose of his visit. Perhaps not entirely the purpose, for I think he was trying to size me up as a man."

"Then let him, for he is a good judge of character, Felix, and so I think you can almost take comfort in his visit."

"Are you really so sure of this man?"

"I cannot explain it, but I warmed to him immediately. I have only been in his company briefly, and yet I had the greatest sense of trust. I liked him very much, and I cannot say that I ordinarily like a person on first meeting."

"You are also good judge of character, so perhaps I will take a little comfort in this for now." He smiled at her, realising that he was trying to swallow down a little jealousy.

Surely, she had not meant that she had a great attraction for this man who was easily old enough to be her father. Why should it matter to him if he did? Was he not the one who had decided to maintain a little distance and not play with that tender heart of hers? And yet when had he really kept his distance? When had he lain down at night without her being his very last thought before sleep?

"That being said, he has been a visitor to Northcott Hall, and Philip did treat him rather well. I would not entirely dismiss the idea that Philip might be feeding Captain Boscowan little suspicions."

"I know Philip is hateful and pernicious, but I am not so sure he would go as far as having me hanged for a smuggler," Felix laughed.

"Not even to save himself?" Clarissa said, her face as serious as he had ever seen it.

"Save himself? What do you mean?"

"A part of everything I had to tell you today was this," she said and paused, seeming a little awkward. "Felix, it is my firmly held belief that somewhere below stairs in Northcott Hall is a Smuggler's hide."

"What?" Felix said, almost letting go of his teacup as he sat forward in his chair. "My brother is a smuggler?"

"I would not go as far as to say that, Felix. What I am saying, what I am certain of, is that he is hiding contraband at Northcott."

"You are a clever woman, Clarissa, so I will not doubt what you say. I will, however, have to ask you how you have come to such a conclusion."

"Some nights ago, I heard your brother's voice in the middle of the night. It was truly the middle of the night, being three o'clock in the morning. I had heard a footstep outside, for I always sleep with my windows open. It startled me and I crept out of my chamber to listen for sounds of an intruder in the house. I heard muffled and indistinct conversation from some distance away and then I heard your brother say, most clearly, that he had a place ready below stairs, but that his companion or companions must be quiet."

"And did you see where they went?"

"No, I dared not risk it. But that is not all," she said hurriedly.

"Oh?"

"My maid, a most trustworthy young woman, told me just yesterday morning how she herself had been awoken the night before, just days after I had been. She had seen a rough and frightening looking man in the darkness, and it was a mercy that he did not see her too. She also heard Philip's voice, but not so clearly as to have discerned his words. And, once again, it was three o'clock; the very dead of night."

Felix turned it all over in his mind, trying to find a way in which his brother, a man who despised him so thoroughly, could be innocent of such an allegation. But why would he be below stairs in the middle of the night with a rough looking stranger? Why would he say he had a place ready? It was a hide, surely.

"I just cannot understand why he would do it, Felix," Clarissa went on when he had been silent for some time. "I cannot understand why he would need to. Philip is so wealthy, surely, he does not need to make money in such a way. He takes such a great risk."

"Ah, but he does not, does he?"

"What do you mean?"

"It is a point you answered yourself just days ago, Clarissa. When we first talked of smuggling and you declared that nobody would surely suspect me, Felix Ravenswood, the son of an earl."

"Oh, I see."

"But whereas they would easily suspect me, the black sheep of the family, nobody would suspect Philip. He is not just the son of the Earl; he is the Earl of Northcott himself. Everybody knows of his wealth; everybody knows of his status. For most of the county, Philip Ravenswood is a man above reproach and always will be. And to have Captain Boscowan himself take tea with you all is the mark of a very confident man."

"Yes, there is no doubt at all that he heard my thorough conversation with Captain Boscowan as we talked of smuggling. Goodness, would his nerves have not at least bristled a little?"

"Arrogance and confidence are as effective as ether in dulling the senses."

"I cannot help but think that Captain Boscowan would, if he spent any length of time in Philip's company, at least find something amiss. You have met him yourself; he is such a man who perceives a thing in a heartbeat. I had not been in his company ten minutes when I realised he knew precisely my circumstances at Northcott Hall, of my taut relationship with Eliza, and even that Philip would have me married to Daniel Morgan. He did not speak of it, but I knew he could see it."

"There is one thing you are unwittingly dismissing, Clarissa."

"And what is that?"

"That Captain Boscowan himself knows very well who is smuggling contraband and who is hiding it in this part of Cornwall."

"You mean…?" she said and looked horrified.

"Yes, there is a chance that Captain Boscowan is in on it."

"Oh, Felix! I do hope not. But if he is, how am I to discover it?"

"You are *not*, Clarissa!" Felix said sternly. "Let your investigations concern my father's diaries and no more. You have already been smart enough to discover that my brother, a man who had likely thought he has been most discreet, is involved in smuggling. For now, I do not think there is anything else to do. You must leave it alone."

"Even if he continues to throw suspicion your way?"

"I thank you for your concern, Clarissa, but I must beg you not to act upon it. We do not yet know that Philip has thrown any suspicion my way, do we? And even if he has, there is no smuggling through Smugglers' Cove anymore."

"Very well," she said, and he hoped that she had heeded his words.

He was beginning to feel very troubled about Clarissa's continued stay at Northcott Hall and he could not bear the idea of her coming to some harm.

Chapter Twenty-Two

Clarissa and Felix had decided not to meet for several days, the idea that Clarissa continually leaving Northcott would bring suspicion at a time when it would be least welcome. But to be at Northcott was difficult now, even more difficult than it had been before, for now she was absolutely certain of Philip's involvement in smuggling. And what of the man she had heard Flo describe so colourfully? Clarissa certainly did not want to come across such a person in the middle of the night.

Clarissa had continued to study the diaries, carefully making her way up to the attic every so often to find herself another. Perhaps she would never have any greater lead than the one she had discovered regarding Carlson, her old guardian's valet. Nonetheless, it soothed her rattled nerves to keep reading, to keep trying, for she most certainly needed a distraction from her fears and the uncertainty at Northcott. Turning her attention away from one little mystery and focusing it upon another was certainly a good distraction indeed. That was, however, until she stumbled across none other than Captain Boscowan on his way out of Northcott.

Clarissa had risen early, taken breakfast with Philip and Eliza for the sake of appearances, and had then enjoyed a brief walk in the gardens. When she had returned, she retired to her room for a little while, reading just a little more of the latest diary. After a while, Clarissa wanted to stretch her legs and decided to walk down to the library and find herself a frivolous sort of novel, if she could find such a thing in amongst the dark bound tomes. She liked the library; it was a quiet place, a place in which she had never been disturbed once since her old guardian had passed away. Philip and Eliza most certainly did not make good use of the books, and she was glad of it.

However, when she walked through the entrance hall and down the corridor which would lead her to the library, Clarissa stopped dead in her tracks. Another door ahead of her opened, the door to Philip's study, and both Philip and Captain Boscowan walked out of it.

"So, I hope that helps," Philip said and clapped the Captain in a rather comradely fashion on the back.

"I am sure it does help, Lord Northcott," the Captain said, turning his attention sharply from his host to look at Clarissa.

She began to walk again, hoping to appear entirely natural. It was a simple enough thing, despite her pounding heart and raging suspicions, when Captain Boscowan smiled at her, clearly pleased to see her.

"Miss Tate, good morning," he said and bowed deeply.

"Good morning, Captain Boscowan. How nice to see you again," Clarissa said, and hoped that it was.

He held her attention for a moment, his smiling eyes meeting hers, that general sense of a sort of fatherly dependability emanating from him. She realised there and then that it would hurt her deeply to discover that he was not the man she had assumed him to be, even though she knew so little of him. He was an easy man to like, but perhaps that was by design rather than nature. She could hardly bear to think of it and look at him at the same time.

"Very well, run along, Clarissa," Philip said with the air of a father who was caught somewhere between patronising her and indulging her like a child.

"Indeed, I am on my way to the library for a while," she said, directing her comment to Captain Boscowan but intending it for Philip, by way of explanation for her sudden presence.

After all, she truly had not known the two men were in the study and she most certainly would not have had the sort of reckless courage required to eavesdrop in broad daylight.

Captain Boscowan bowed once again before the two men took their leave of her and continued through the corridor towards the entrance hall and the main door.

With her insides shaking, Clarissa hurried on into the library, opening the door, scurrying inside, and closing it behind her. She leaned her back against the door, wondering why it was she was so breathless, and spent a moment or two trying to regain control. Nothing frightening had happened, and yet here her heart was pounding like a drum, racing like a skittish horse. Perhaps it was the idea that the odds were stacked against Felix, a realisation that, even if Captain Boscowan was not a part of it, Philip was most certainly feeding him the sort of information, *fictional information*, that could well cause his brother harm.

"So, I hope that helps." Philip's words to the Captain in those moments before they realised her presence ricocheted off the walls of her skull like a bullet in a steel box.

Clarissa knew she could interpret that in a number of ways, and none of them good. Had he given Captain Boscowan some allegedly vital piece of information which he hoped would help? Or had the two of them simply been discussing the hide, a handy and secret place for two men *above reproach* to store illicit goods? Was that what he hoped had helped? Of course, it could be something else altogether, something innocent, but Clarissa could not, in her current state, begin to imagine what that might be.

Clarissa slumped down at the large rectangular mahogany reading desk, resting her elbows heavily upon it and her chin in her hands. What if Philip really had given the Captain some falsehood, some little lie that would truly edge his own brother towards the gallows? She felt hot and sick; even if Captain Boscowan was a good man and not involved in all of this, could Felix be, in some way, made to look like a real smuggler? Could this be done so convincingly? But surely that would suggest pure hatred; the very purist hatred. And what on earth had Felix ever done to Philip, his own brother, to have him hate him so much? Surely this was more than a little masculine rivalry between brothers! This went deeper, like everything in the Ravenswood family. Did it go so deep as to touch the edges of the old Earl's secret?

It seemed to Clarissa that there was now mystery all around her, that there was some overlap that she could not see. She no longer had two distinct set of circumstances that she could split to better aid her focus on one or the other; for some reason, that simple sentence spoken by Lord Northcott had somehow joined them, making them one in a way which did not make sense to her. She just felt it.

For the rest of the day, Clarissa had the deepest sense that Felix was in some trouble. She still could not define it, she still could not explain it, but she knew she would never forgive herself if she did not take some action. Perhaps it was her recent feelings of freedom and complete autonomy that the old Earl had given which had made her a different woman. Perhaps now she was the sort of woman who would not stand on the edge of events and hope that the decency and inherent goodness of men would prevail.

Knowing that she would not sleep, Clarissa still retired to her chamber early. She had a plan in mind, a ridiculous, reckless, foolish plan, but one she could not ignore. Felix had once called her courageous, in fact it was a compliment he had paid her more than once. Was she really courageous? Was she courageous enough to do what she was certain must be done?

Deciding that she was, although feeling it in an intellectual rather than an emotional way, Clarissa, dressed in a dark, thick, somewhat utilitarian old gown, old walking boots and, carrying a small oil lamp, silently crept out of Northcott Hall before midnight.

She had it in mind to hide out in the woodland and see if anybody approached in the dead of night, hoping to capture a snippet of information that she might take to the authorities, even if she could not confidently take it to Captain Boscowan. She felt curiously relieved to reach the dark woodland, even though the very idea of being out in such a place alone at night would ordinarily have terrified her. But Clarissa was glad to have made it, to have escaped from the house without being seen by anybody. She hovered in the woods for a while, putting a match finally to the oil lamp but keeping it burning very low, barely lighting her way at all. It was just enough so that she could make her way to the safety of the middle without falling.

After half an hour of waiting, Clarissa began to wonder if she had truly thought this through. What evidence was it really to see a man approaching the hall, even if he was carrying something, some well packed contraband? She could not approach such a man and she could never truly say that she knew what he had carried. Everything could be explained away, and Felix would still be in danger.

With a sigh, she had almost considered making her way back into the hall. That was until a thought occurred to her; perhaps a man walking towards the hall carrying something was not firm evidence, but what if she had seen men on the shore, handing parcels wrapped in waterproof oil skin up from boats? That was something that could not be quite so easily explained, especially if she surreptitiously followed those men all the way back to Northcott Hall. Surely her testimony would be enough then, would not it?

Clarissa knew it was foolhardy, and she knew that she had never been more afraid, but she thought of Felix and how easily the county had believed such simple rumours that had been begun by his own brother. What a simple thing it would be to expand those rumours, to have the greatest suspicion turn those rumours into facts in the minds of all.

She hurried through the woodland and made her way off the Northcott estate, turning the oil lamp down completely and navigating her way by the pale moonlight alone. Clarissa did not want her tiny light to be seen out in the middle of the peninsula, not when there were soldiers in the area.

She was breathless and uncomfortably hot by the time she reached smugglers' Cove and peered down, wondering if all was well below. If only the cove could be seen in its entirety from her vantage point, then she could be sure that there was no boat silently moored, fooling even the master of Farwynnen House himself.

Without another thought, Clarissa embarked upon that steep slope down. It was so dark that she had to stop and light the little oil lamp once again. She carefully made her way to the bottom, knowing that she would not rest easy until she had seen with her own eyes that the cove was empty of unwanted visitors. When the moon appeared from behind some thick cloud, the cove was lit enough for her to see that there was nothing there at all; no boat, no men, no danger.

She turned and hurried back up that pathway, breathing hard as her legs pumped, her muscles burning a little with the effort of climbing such a steep incline with such haste.

The moment she reached the coastal path again, she hurriedly extinguished the oil lamp. She looked north and south along the peninsula in the muted moonlight, her eyes desperately trying to focus for any sign of soldiers. Seeing nothing, she turned her attention to the sea, but it simply looked black and she was certain she would never see a boat on it at all unless it carried its own light. The chances of smugglers doing such a thing were remote, and so she was left to wonder what her next move would be.

Clarissa had a choice to make, and she made it with speed. She would continue south along the coastal path, peering down wherever she could get a good sight, hoping to finally see something of note, even if the idea of it frightened her to the very core of her being.

She picked up speed, moving faster and faster, her breath stinging her throat as it dried it. It was not until she had walked another mile, almost reaching Gribben Head, that she heard something in the distance. It was just a suspicion of voices on the air, and there being no houses, no buildings, not even a shepherd's hut in that area, she knew the sound must be coming from below; from the shore.

She finally reached the very bottom end of the peninsula, sliding down a narrow track, no care for how the dusty ground and ancient rocks were spoiling her gown. Clarissa just continued to pick her way down, stopping every so often to hide behind a cluster of rocks, peering out to see what she could see below.

Finally, she had the view that she had been waiting for; the thing she had both hoped for and feared. There was a rowing boat on the shore, a long wooden gig, half on the sand, half in the shallow water, and four were men working to empty it. She could not make out the faces, but her mind would not let go of the idea that the ugly man Flo had described was among them. The man who looked as if he would knock you to the ground and eat the skin off your face whilst you were unconscious. She shivered, wondering what she should do next.

Could she stay where she was? Hidden in that little outcrop of rocks? But what if the men made their way up that narrow track? Would they not just find her and throw her into the sea? She knew that smugglers could be desperate, violent men; men who would stick at nothing to save their own necks, for it was a hanging offence.

Clarissa felt a horrible prickling of fear, deciding that she would turn and make her way back, at least to try to find some other hiding place that was more secure. But before she had a chance to turn, she was seized roughly from behind, a big hand clamped over her mouth and an arm encircling her waist, lifting her off her feet and carrying her away.

Clarissa was absolutely terrified and her instinct for survival strong. She would wait until the man put her down and swing her oil lamp at his face, hoping to stun him for just long enough for her to make her escape. But when the man pulled her into a cave that she had not seen on her way down, her heart sank. How would she escape him now, even if she managed to hit him with her lamp?

"Clarissa, it is Felix," he said, breathing the words into her ear almost silently.

She relaxed a little, unable to entirely take in the full circumstances but knowing she was surely safe in his arms. Whatever this meant, even if Felix Ravenswood was a smuggler, she was certain that he would not kill her. She nodded slowly, indicating that he might now take his hand from her mouth and let her go; she would not scream. She turned, but she could see nothing. She knew he was there; she could feel him, even though they were now not touching.

She pulled the matches from the pocket of her gown and struck one, the flare shaking in the darkness in her hands. She tried to light the lamp, but her hands would not stay still, and the match finely went out.

"Give me the matches," Felix whispered again.

In no time at all, he had the lamp lit and pulled her deeper into the narrow cave.

"What on earth are you doing here, Clarissa Tate?" he said, and sounded absolutely furious with her.

"Felix, I am so sorry. Please forgive me, I did not come here to trap you. I never realised for a moment that you were one of the smugglers and, even if I had, I do not think I could have found it in my heart to have given you away." Tears were rolling down her face.

"One of the smugglers?" he said, his incredulity clear even though he was whispering.

"Are you not a smuggler? Are you not with those men below?"

"No, I am not with those men below," he said without a hint of amusement. "I am the man who saw a lamplight on my cove and sought to follow it. I presume that was you," he said and paused long enough for her to respond.

"Yes," she said feebly.

"At first, I thought perhaps a soldier, but they would not be so sneaky. Believing that I had somebody scoping out my cove with a view to smuggling something in tonight, I came out immediately and gave chase. You must have been moving at some speed, Clarissa, because I did not catch up with you until Gribben Head. When I saw you hiding behind those rocks, that was when I realised it was you. Well, it was a woman in a gown. What other woman would be foolish enough to come out here in the dead of night and spy on such desperate men? I have never been angrier than I am now," he said, and although his voice was quiet, it frightened her; she did not need to hear his anger, she could feel it.

"Felix, you do not understand. This morning, Captain Boscowan…" Felix quietened her suddenly by placing a finger over her lips and leaving it there, gently leaning it against her skin.

"They are on the move, Clarissa. They are making their way up from the shore." He leaned in close, his lips on her ear as he spoke in the quietest whisper.

"What should we do?" she said, terrified once again.

"Turn down that lamp and pray they do not use this cave, that is what," he said mercilessly.

As they stood there in the darkness, that cold, miserable, narrow cave, Clarissa wished that she could lean against him, to feel his strength and to be comforted by it. She strained to listen, hearing feet on the path and muted conversation.

She did not need to strain to hear as the men, or at least two of them, walked past the very mouth of the cave, just feet away from where she stood. She held her breath, as if they would hear her breathing and discover them.

"Come on, let's get a move on. I want to get this lot to *Norffcott* before this place is teeming with soldiers again. They're like bleedin' ants, they are; crawling every bleedin' where!" the man's voice was rough, aggressive, and very clearly not Cornish.

It was a voice she would not easily forget, a deep, aggressive tone that must surely belong to a big, ugly man. The accent reminded her entirely of the rough and blunt way that the poorest in London spoke. She had only ever been there once in her life, but that accent was something she would never forget; so harsh when compared with her beloved Cornish. *Norffcott*, that was how he had pronounced it. No Cornishman, rich or poor, would have pronounced it such.

"I think we are safe," Felix whispered into her ear and she could hear the relief in his voice.

"We have to follow them back to the hall, Felix. That was my plan," Clarissa said and turned as if to do just that, just as Felix had crouched to turn up the oil lamp a little, throwing a barely discernible yellow light in that dark cave.

Felix rose, gripping her by the shoulders and pulling her back into the cave, so furiously that she almost fell. Clarissa drew in her breath and stared back at him wide-eyed, their faces just inches apart.

"Felix!" she hissed.

"You cannot go out there! For God's sake, can you not see how foolish and dangerous it is?" He was breathing heavily, his eyes so black in that darkness, so furious with her. "Have you not put yourself in enough danger tonight? And what would you gain now? What would it prove to follow them all the way back to Northcott Hall? You heard with your own ears as I did that *that* is where they are going, so what was your intention? Did you plan to confront them on the steps of my brother's house and hope that they not kill you? And what about the soldiers?"

"I did not see any on my way here," she said, trying to defend herself but realising that her behaviour was, perhaps, a little indefensible.

"And you think that means they are not there? You expect to see bright red jackets gleaming in the moonlight? Soldiers neatly marching towards you as they might by day? For God's sake, Clarissa!" His breathing was so hard now that his breath was coming in angry snorts. "If I am found now out here having followed you, what will that mean? Especially if those two making their way to Northcott now are caught on the peninsular. If they are caught and I am caught, even your glorious Captain Boscowan will see me hanged!"

"Oh Felix, I had not thought of it. But I had not thought you would be here; I would never put you in danger."

"I know you would not, Clarissa," he said, the anger subsiding a little as exasperation and exhaustion took over. "But you would not think long and hard before putting yourself in danger, would you? You could have been killed tonight, Clarissa. They would not look at you as a woman, even as a lady. They would have beaten you to death with their fists and their boots and they would have thrown your body into the sea. Think about that," he said, and turned from her, running his hands through his hair and clearly thinking about that very thing himself.

Without warning, he turned back to her suddenly, seizing her shoulders once more only this time he drew her towards him. Before Clarissa knew what was happening, his lips were on hers, pressing hard against her, her back finding the jagged wall of the cave. Her head was spinning, and her heart pounding hard. Their emotions were so heightened that this seemed to be the only way to release them and Clarissa realised that she was feeling that same sense of relief herself. The fear, the excitement, the pain of her argument with the man she knew she had fallen in love with, it was all gone in that moment. Everything was gone, the cave, the night, her purpose; there was nothing but Felix.

Clarissa reached for him, her hands finding his face, her palms lying flat against his smooth, dark skin. He kissed her with great passion, a passion that Clarissa returned. Just as she felt herself beginning to spiral into a world she had never known before, Felix took his hands from her, placed them on of the cave wall either side of her head, and forcibly pushed himself away from her.

"Forgive me," he said, his voice hoarse and rough; gravelly.

"Felix, I do not need to forgive you," she began. "Felix?"

"Then it is for me to forgive myself," he said, a little of his anger returning but she thought, on this occasion, it was for himself and no longer her.

"Felix, please,"

"I should not have behaved in that way, Clarissa. I shall not excuse my actions on the excitement of the evening, the fear, the anger. But I shall keep to my side of the cave tonight and you must keep to yours."

"Tonight?" Clarissa said, wondering if he meant to keep her there.

"Do not sound afraid. You have no need to be afraid of me, despite my actions. But listen, we cannot stride out across the peninsular now. Whether you like it or not, we will have to wait it out here in the dark until the day is not only broken but established. We must not look suspicious, out of place. The soldiers should be at rest by then or patrolling without any expectation of finding anything. Then I will walk my way and you will walk yours. Separate, without suspicion. It is the only way, Clarissa, for there will be no explanation for either one of us if we are caught tonight."

"You are quite right, Felix. I really am so sorry for this, every bit of it. Please believe me that I did it with the best of intentions. Captain Boscowan was at Northcott this morning, and I had the greatest sense that Philip had told him something, some lie that would see you in trouble or danger. I know my plan was not a sensible one, and God knows I am terrified, for I have never done anything so dangerous and frightening in my life, but my motive was true, as is my apology."

"I know," he said, his voice a whisper once again. "I know."

Chapter Twenty-Three.

Clarissa wandered back through the Northcott Estate woodland boldly, just in case she was seen. There must be nothing furtive about her movements, not if she was to avoid suspicion and have anyone who asked her believe that she had been walking.

She ached from head to foot, her hour or two of broken sleep as she had leaned against the hard walls of the cave something that she would certainly suffer from for days.

Clarissa felt so unusual, she could hardly work it out. In the cold light of day, her actions really had been foolish. However, they had also confirmed everything she had suspected, and she knew that those two men had made their way to Northcott last night and that the contraband had been hidden away somewhere below stairs. She had witnessed it, and so had Felix. However, if Captain Boscowan was not an ally, then what would her testimony be worth if she admitted to being there with Felix Ravenswood? It was all too much to think about, especially when she was so exhausted.

Clarissa finally walked into Northcott Hall, so hungry that she would have given anything for breakfast but knowing that Eliza and Philip were likely already in there, and her appearance was far from tidy. Her heart sank, however, as she made her way to the foot of the stairs so that she might hasten up to her chamber and quickly wash and dress, for Eliza herself was wafting down the great staircase, looking her up and down with a mixture of contempt and confusion.

"What a sight you look!" Eliza said, not bothering to be polite about it. "What on earth have you been up to?"

"I woke very early this morning, Lady Northcott, and thought to have a walk to give myself an appetite for breakfast." Clarissa hoped she sounded convincing. "Anyway, I got a little diverted and found myself walking all the way down to Polridmouth Cove, where I lost my footing and fell rather awkwardly. I fear I have ruined this gown," she added and gave a rueful smile.

Polridmouth Cove was clear on the other side of the peninsular, a place which stared across the River Fowey to Polruan, a good distance away from where she had truly been.

"You were not hurt, I trust?" Eliza said, remembering to feign concern; remembering that, for whatever reason, she needed to be kind, she needed to keep her here, she needed her to marry Daniel Morgan.

"Perhaps a pulled muscle or two, but nothing serious. Thank you, Lady Northcott," Clarissa said and bowed her head respectfully. "Perhaps I ought to tidy myself up though, before I take breakfast," she added with a smile.

"Yes, indeed," Eliza nodded and then passed her, making her way to the breakfast room.

After tidying herself and taking breakfast, Clarissa made her way back to her chamber for some much-needed rest. She was utterly exhausted; she knew she must sleep and sleep she did. Having no idea how long she had been there, Clarissa was entirely unconscious until she was shaken gently awake, opening her eyes and slowly focusing upon the pretty little face of Flo Pettigrew.

"Forgive me, Miss," Flo said in a gentle tone as if she were waking a baby.

"What is it, Flo?" Clarissa slowly sat up. "Is everything all right?"

"I think you might have slept the day away, Miss," Flo was smiling at her, a little amused. "But Her Ladyship has sent me up to find you, Miss. It is almost time for afternoon tea, and she wants you to join them."

"Oh, very well," Clarissa said and rose to her feet, shaking out her gown and wondering if it would pass muster, even though she had spent the last few hours asleep in it.

"There is something else, Miss," Flo said tentatively.

"What?"

"Her Ladyship did not say anything about it, but I saw him with my own eyes."

"Who? Where?" Sleep still held her and she was feeling confused, struggling to concentrate properly.

"I passed the open door of the drawing room, Daniel Morgan was already in there," she had lowered her voice to a whisper and looked over her shoulder, almost as if she expected to see the Countess herself standing behind her. "But you must not say anything, Miss. Her ladyship never mentioned it and I do not expect she would be very pleased to know I have."

"Have no fear, Flo, I shall look suitably surprised when I see Mr Morgan in front of me," she said with a sigh.

"I reckon we had better change your gown, Miss," Flo went on. "'Tis a little bit rumpled, that one."

By the time Clarissa walked into the drawing room, the tea tray had already arrived. Eliza scowled at her, either from force of habit or because she had perceived what her husband had not; Clarissa would never marry Daniel Morgan.

"Ah, Clarissa," Philip said, with such warmth that Clarissa's eyes opened wide.

"Forgive me for being late, Lord Northcott." She turned to look at Daniel Morgan. "Mr Morgan, I hope you are well. I hope you will forgive me, sir, for I took a tumble this morning when I was out and I have been nursing my injuries ever since." She smiled, making sure it never reached her eyes.

Daniel Morgan, who had jumped to his feet the moment Clarissa had walked into the room, bowed deeply. He straightened up and smiled at her, that dreadful oily smile she had first seen at Lord and Lady Sedgwick's ball.

"I hope you are not too injured, Miss Tate?" he said, his concern entirely cosmetic.

"Just a bruise and a scratch, a few aches and pains, but nothing very serious, I thank you," she said and took a seat, smiling at Eliza and she did so.

"My, this tea looks very inviting," Daniel Morgan said, and Eliza turned to look sharply at the maid who was waiting patiently and silently next to the door.

She hurried over and began to pour tea for them all, as Clarissa looked on. How different things were here, and not necessarily for the better. This poor maid looked terrified, nervously pouring tea that she hoped she did not spill under the unforgiving, merciless gaze of her mistress, the countess. She could not help but think of Bess Pengelly, waddling about, her rotund frame nipped in at the middle by a long white apron. Her round face, smiling eyes, and that wonderful way she humorously maintained some form of mock exasperation with the master of the house. She tried to imagine the same thing at Northcott and found herself smiling.

"I must admit, Miss Tate, you do look rather well despite your fall," Daniel said, smiling back at her.

"Oh, thank you," she said awkwardly, hoping that he had not thought her amused smile was meant for him.

"I hope your injuries will not prevent you dancing at Sir William Treglown's summer ball next week?" he went on, that determinedly clipped way of speaking he had grating on her nerves.

She had never heard anybody speak quite like that before and she wondered, idly, just where exactly in Bodmin he hailed from.

"Oh, I had not realised Sir William was hosting a ball, you have taken me by surprise, Mr Morgan," Clarissa was trying her hardest to be polite without being effusive.

She had become more and more sensitive to the idea of being discovered in some way, either for her determined study of the last Earl's most private diaries, or for the greater crime of being out in the darkness as smugglers brought contraband ashore and delivered it to Northcott itself. Just the idea of tobacco, silk, and lace, wrapped in oilskin packets somewhere below stairs, made her shiver.

"Are you all right, Clarissa?" Philip said, once again treating her to a display of concern he did not feel.

"Yes, I think I must have given myself a little shock this morning when I fell and it is feeble of me, I know, but I seem to be struggling to get over it." she said and saw both Eliza and Daniel Morgan nod approvingly; she was feeble, she was weak, she was just what she ought to be.

If only they had realised that she had crept from this house in the dark, across the peninsular alone, and spied upon desperate criminals as they brought their illicit goods ashore. Perhaps they might not think her quite so feeble then.

"It is perfectly understandable, Clarissa." Eliza was smiling at her.

"Perhaps a little fresh air, Miss Tate? I would be honoured to escort you," Daniel Morgan said hopefully; that oily smile, those ridiculously high collars! Would he never desist?

"Forgive me, I think I have had perhaps a little too much fresh air. I suppose I ought not to have wandered so far before breakfast," she was playing their game, but she hated it.

She had to remind herself that she was just keeping them at bay, avoiding their suspicion, that was all. She was already almost entirely sure that she would not be attending the summer ball at the home of Sir William Treglown the following week, where was the harm in a little pretence?

"If you are sure," Daniel Morgan said and looked a little crestfallen.

"I do not want to have to attend another ball in which I cannot dance, Mr Morgan," Clarissa laughed prettily, and everybody present seemed to be brightened by her own mood.

They all thought she was coming around; this stupid feeble girl, without family or guardian, ready to throw herself onto the path of the pasty-faced man. Well, let them think that.

Chapter Twenty-Four

As Clarissa made her way to Mrs Nancarrow's home for the bridge afternoon just two days later, her visit served two distinct purposes. For one, it added a sense of normality, her everyday interests and excursions being followed to the letter, no need for suspicion. For another, she was certain that Felix would be there, and she needed to speak to him desperately.

Clarissa had stuck rigidly to the determination they had made between them not to see one another for a little while. As hard as it had been, especially when she had made her newest discovery, she would not go against him this time. He had been so angry with her in the cave that night, and although her mission had served its purpose, if she had not been dragged into that cave by him, she might well have been beaten to death with fist and foot just as Felix had so sharply explained.

So, she had decided to hope he would be in Mrs Nancarrow's drawing-room and that Lady Marchmont would find a way to put the two of them together in private for at least a few minutes.

Mrs Nancarrow had, as always, been pleased to see her. Clarissa determined that, if she could have an early encounter with Felix, she would most certainly spend a little time at the bridge tables that afternoon, the very reason for which she was invited. She felt she owed it to Mrs Nancarrow, an unwitting facilitator to her secret friendship with Felix.

"Oh, I am so glad you came," Lady Marchmont said, greeting her with her customary warmth of squeezed hands and a kissed cheek.

"Is he here?" Clarissa whispered, her eyes furtive.

"Of course, he is. How could he stay away?" Lady Marchmont looked mischievous.

"Forgive me, Lady Marchmont, but you must come up with some clever way to put Felix and I together privately, just for a matter of five minutes and no more at some point this afternoon."

"Of course, my dear. Consider it done," Gwendolyn Marchmont did not need an explanation; the very fact that she had been asked to arrange something a little scandalous was enough excitement for her.

"Thank you," Clarissa said and breathed a sigh of relief.

"Just promise me that you are safe. Not from Felix, of course, but *safe*. You know what I mean. *At Northcott*." She mouthed the last.

"Yes, I think I am. For now, at least. But I am vigilantly watching for changes; I shall not unwittingly put myself at risk."

"You do *believe* there is a risk, I can see it in your eyes."

"Perhaps, but I truly do not know. But I think to rule it out would be foolish on my part, and so I cannot."

"Very well, I shall trust you and Felix to know the right thing to do. In the meantime, the three of us will walk down to Mrs Nancarrow's beautiful camellia garden, where you and Felix can have five minutes alone. Will that do?"

"It is perfect, Lady Marchmont."

"Very well, now, just let me draw him out."

True to her word, Lady Marchmont had left the two of them alone in the camellia garden. She had not made her way back to the house, but she had lingered far enough away that she would not overhear them. Something about that had pleasantly surprised Clarissa, for she had erroneously assumed that Gwendolyn Marchmont would be no stranger to a little eavesdropping, albeit rather harmless. She felt a little shabby when she realised that she had done her friend a silent disservice.

"Clarissa, I am so glad you came." Felix spoke quietly, his dark eyes on hers, his hair, even as it was tied back in its neat black ribbon, lifting on the gentle breeze coming in from the rolling sea.

"I have much to tell you, Felix, and we do not have long," she said, pulling the small diary from the pocket of her gown.

"Well, before you begin, at least let me apologise for the other night. I shall not apologise for my anger or the things I said to you, for I meant them at the time, although I would never hurt and upset you for the world. But I think you must know that I am apologising for my advances; they were ungentlemanly and rough." He was looking at her earnestly, without a hint of embarrassment, just genuine regret.

Clarissa did not want him to regret it; she did not want to regret it herself. She wanted to remember that kiss for the rest of her life and she did not want it to be the first and only time she would ever experience such passion in his arms.

"Felix, please do not apologise. I am not offended; I was not offended at the time. How I wish I had time for us to talk more about this, for I would not have you feel awkward and I would never have you feel that you were anything but a gentleman. But there is not time, Felix, because I have found it," she said and held the diary up in front of her. "I have found it."

Clarissa was still reeling from the moment, at midnight the night before, when she had finally found the most revealing passage yet in her old guardian's diaries. She had almost rolled out of bed with shock, finally falling asleep clutching the little volume to her chest, never releasing it lest something happen to make it disappear. She had carried it in her pocket at breakfast, and she had never let it out of her sight.

"Read it to me," he said, and she wished he had not; what if somebody were to overhear them?

Clarissa looked all around her, seeing no sign of anybody but Gwendolyn Marchmont in the distance.

"6ᵗʰ June 1784

My wife is gone, and everything is lost. When Jennifer was still with me, there was a hope for the future, a futile idea that we would be able to recover from this and keep going. But as of this morning, that hope is gone. Extinguished, just as the life was extinguished from Jennifer's eyes. Dead, and by her own hand; but is it not really by mine? Why did I let my fear overcome me? Why did I think that I was helping? It was such a foolish thing to do, such an ill-conceived plan, and I believe that, in the end, my foolish actions, actions which now cannot be taken back, were the very thing which finally drove her into the arms of death. I have seen her slowly withering these last few months and I should have known that she could not take any more. I should have been with her every moment, never once leaving her alone for long enough that she might tie a cord around her neck and choke away her own life.

She has been dying slowly, bit by bit, every day forced to cradle child who is not hers. I saw immediately how it tortured her soul and forbade her the grieving that should have been her right. For how can a mother grieve for her lost child when she has another in her arms and all the world thinks it to be hers? What I thought of as a kindness was, in the end, a dreadful, unimaginable torture. I had thought I knew better, my own heart broken, but thinking that I must do anything to wipe away her pain. But perhaps that pain is not supposed to be wiped away, covered over, hidden. I realise now it is to be felt, experienced, that rawness, that desperation for things to be how they once were. That is grief; it is the natural way of things, and I interfered. I put a stop to the natural way of things and, as a result, silently, lovingly, and foolishly pushed my own wife from this world and into the next. What is there to do now but grieve? But should I really allow myself the painful luxury that I did not allow my wife? Can a man be forgiven for a decision made in a moment and executed in just a matter of days? Oh, if I could go back, I would have buried my boy properly and held my wife in my arms in full view of his mourners. But that will never happen, will it? I have no wife; I have no child. All I have is a lifelong responsibility to the tiny stranger who will, one day, be the Earl of Northcott. Well, let that be my punishment."

When she finished, Clarissa looked up into his face. Felix's mouth hung open and his eyes were full of amazement. He was shaken, she could see that much, and she heartily wished that they could have done this within the safety of the wonderful, beautiful, dark medieval walls of Farwynnen House.

"Felix?" she said gently, looking over her shoulder before looking back at him. "That is it, that is the secret. You have it at last."

"I know," he said, staring at her but not really focusing.

"You know who the dead child is, the baby he buried, do you not?" she said, suddenly not sure he had taken in the full ramifications.

"Philip. Philip Ravenswood, my brother. But who on earth is the man in Northcott Hall?"

"I think we must speak to your father's old valet now."

"Yes, with this diary in my hand, Carlson cannot deny me the full facts."

"Let me come with you, Felix, let me be by your side when you speak to him."

Felix did not respond in words, he simply stared into her eyes and nodded slowly.

Chapter Twenty-Five

Felix and Clarissa met early the following morning, agreeing to rendezvous in the woodland on the east of the estate just a few hundred yards from the cottage where Carlson lived. At first, Felix was not entirely sure that his decision to allow Clarissa to come with him had been the right one, for it was so much closer to Northcott itself and he could not bear the idea of putting her in danger. But what danger could they be in by daylight and from whom? Philip Ravenswood, or whoever he was, would not be surrounded by his smuggling fraternity in the day, and he had certainly never been a physical match for Felix. And, in the end, he knew that Clarissa deserved to be there; she deserved to hear every part of the tale if, indeed, Francis Carlson finally gave it.

If it had not been for Clarissa and her unwavering but gentle tenacity, Felix would have spent the rest of his life wondering why his father had behaved as he had done towards his mother, and why it was he had never allowed himself the simple pleasure of falling in love with Morwenna Roscarrock.

Felix had been relieved to arrive back at Farwynnen the previous afternoon when he had left Mrs Nancarrow's house. He was more relieved still when he remembered that Bess Pengelly would not be there; her husband was having one of his episodes and Felix was to fend for himself for the day.

And so, once he had painstakingly stabled his horse and closed everything up for the evening, Felix had sat himself down on the faded Oriental rug in that curious entrance hall, stared up at the portrait of his beloved mother, and cried. He cried for his mother, he cried for the confused boy he had once been, he cried for the loss of the friendship he could have had with his father. But more than any of that, he cried for the old Earl himself. He had done something reckless, perhaps even from his own poor judgement in grief, but whatever had truly happened, he had spent his entire life paying for it. He had suffered every day and he had denied himself the happiness of allowing life to continue. What an awful thing to live with such guilt, especially when his actions had begun as something meant to soothe the wife he had clearly loved so dearly.

It was a tragedy, all of it, every bit of it. He could even see the tragedy of Philip's life, for who on earth was he? Where did he really belong? No wonder his father had said in his final breaths, *"Do not be unkind to Philip, it is not his fault."* How those words made sense to him as he stared up at his mother's face and cried.

But Philip had been cruel. Not only to Felix, but to Felix's mother also. He had been a rotten youth and a worse man. Could Felix really forgive him for that? And what if Philip really did now seek to have him hanged as a smuggler? If that really was true, how could that be forgiven? Of all the secrets, lies, and tragedies, the only person who had been so determinedly spiteful and cruel had been the man he had thought all these years to be his brother.

"Which cottage is it?" Clarissa said, lightly tapping his arm and dragging him back into the present.

"It is all one cottage, Clarissa. It used to be two, but it is now knocked into one and Carlson has the place to himself."

"I see," Clarissa nodded thoughtfully. "Well, are you ready?"

"Yes, I am ready."

"And you are all right?" she went on and reached out a hand to lightly stroke his cheek before withdrawing it.

"I am," he said and smiled before briefly laying a hand on her shoulder. "Come, let us get this over with."

Francis Carlson, despite being a frail man in his seventies, recognised Felix immediately. He smiled at him, throwing the door open wide and ushering the two of them into his neat, clean little sitting-room.

"This is lovely, Mr Carlson," Clarissa said and Felix smiled himself; she certainly knew how to treat everybody with respect.

"One of the maids comes over from the hall once a week, you know, just to give the place a bit of a once-over. That was His Lordship's thoughtfulness, for he arranged it all, Miss. Never wanted me to go without anything, he didn't," he said and lowered himself tentatively into a seat.

Felix and Clarissa sat side-by-side on a small brown couch opposite him, and Felix felt suddenly grateful to have her so close by. What a woman she was; what an absolute surprise to have found her to be the person he had come to know since his father was so ill. She was a quiet woman, one whom nobody would ever suspect of the bravery, recklessness, and absolute determination to always do what was right, whatever it cost her. Others would dismiss her as a pleasant, beautiful, modestly clever young woman. Those others would, of course, be underestimating her entirely.

"So, what brings you here today, sir?" Carlson said, but there was a look in his eye which suggested to Felix he already had a good idea.

"How is your eyesight, Mr Carlson?" Felix began gently, for he knew well that his father's old valet could read and write very skilfully.

"I can still see, sir," the old man let out a raspy laugh.

"Here, let me point out a passage in this diary here of my father's and ask you to read it," Felix said, having already decided before they had arrived that this would be the best way to begin.

He crossed the room and crouched at Francis Carlson's side, opening the book and handing it to him, pointing at the very entry he wanted him to read.

The man's shoulders fell immediately, and continued to fall as he silently read his way through from one end the other.

"Well, it is true, sir," Carlson said, his eyes still fixed on the page. "And His Lordship was right, I did suffer on account of it. It was kind of him to see it; to know what it had cost me to help him. Oh, and it did cost me too, for it has haunted me for more than thirty years."

"Mr Carlson, we know that Philip Ravenswood, the real Philip Ravenswood, died when he was still just a baby. We know that his father buried him, and we know that he replaced him with the man everybody believes to be the real son and heir to Northcott." Clarissa's voice was gentle and full of compassion. "But we do not know where that new baby came from, nor do we know where the real Philip Ravenswood was buried. You must understand that we do not seek to cause you any trouble, sir, but we must know. Felix must know where his real brother was laid to rest."

"I do not fear trouble, Miss, not at my age, not after all these years. I knew this day would come, a part of me hoped that it would. I know Lord Northcott was almost dead inside from the guilt he had carried over what we had done, and I was not far behind him. Perhaps this is a blessing, to be allowed to admit my sin whilst I still walk the Earth. Well, I will leave nothing out and you may send anybody to my door, I will speak the truth."

"Thank you, Carlson, I am very grateful," Felix said, patting the man on the back before returning to the couch to sit down beside Clarissa.

"Well, little baby Philip did not last long in his world. He was only five months old when he passed away suddenly one night. If the first Lady Northcott had not been such a determined mother, it would have been a nurse who found him. But that poor young woman found him herself, and the Earl told me that he had never seen such grief. He said that her cries were painful enough to tear the world in two, and he reckoned he knew there and then that he would have to do something to stop the pain. Well, I reckon I went along with it. He was always a good man, you see, and I couldn't imagine that he would ever do something that didn't turn out to be for the best." Francis Carlson stopped for a moment and cleared his throat. "But when His Lordship and I buried that child out on the estate, I never thought I would recover from it. The deed was done then; that little pathway which we both agreed to walk was something we already each had a foot on."

"Where is he buried?" Clarissa said gently.

"In the grounds of Northcott, I will never forget it. He is laid to rest where the woodland on the west of the estate meets the boundary wall. His Lordship could hardly bear it, laying that child in the ground so far away from the hall. I think he couldn't bear the thought of that little baby out there alone. But you will find the place if you look, for his Lordship set out his own memorial, in place of a headstone, you understand. He'd gathered some pebbles from down on the shore and he set them on top of that grave in the shape of a cross."

"What did you do then? After the baby was buried?" Felix asked.

"His Lordship sent me out to find a young woman in some need. I knew what he meant, I have known him since he was barely a man and we did not need to say much between us to be understood. And so, I made my way along the coast, far enough away as would make no difference. Ended up in Talland, I did, and quickly found a little gossip. You know how folks love to give such details of other's lives, not to mention their own ugly judgements. Well, I found a young woman, not a kid, mind you, but a sensible woman of three-and-twenty. She was a late-starter but had been due to marry her beau just a week before the young man died in the copper mine. Drowned, he did, when he fell into a watery pit in the darkness," he shook his head sadly. "Anyway, her condition soon became obvious to all, the condition she had never thought would be discovered. They were to be married after all, and they wouldn't be the first to be a little premature in celebrating their nuptials, as it were," he said and looked apologetically at Clarissa. "When she had the baby, the poor woman was shunned. Left to survive on nothing in a wooden shack with hardly a roof on it. And left by her own family, too! As if we don't all come into this world in the same way! What fools we are."

"Poor Lucy," Felix said, for he now knew it was she; had Marjorie Ames not said she hailed from Talland? It was beginning to fall into place.

"Aye, sir, it was Lucy. Poor Lucy Bates. Still, she was glad enough to have a position in a fine home and the chance to still raise her own child, even though she was never to tell the boy who he really was. Had she stayed in that shack, the pair of them would have died the first hard winter to come along. I know it's no fine thing to find excuses for myself and believe me I am not. It's just the truth, plain and simple."

"How did she manage? Seeing her baby every day and never able to tell him who she was?" Clarissa took over.

"Quite well, for the first few years. Better still when the new Lady Northcott came and there was another baby to care for too. She was in her element. But you're right to wonder, for it did get to her in the end. The young Master Philip was a cruel and arrogant child, may God forgive me for saying it, and it only worsened as he grew. He was an aristocrat in his ways if he was not in his blood, and he treated that poor woman like a fool. He talked to her in a way that no mother should have to suffer, until one day, she just told him. It broke out of her, so His Lordship told me, and she declared him to be Arnold Bates, her own child and not the heir to Northcott at all. Well, he confronted his father and, for the first time in all those years, he told the truth. His wife had killed herself, his second wife languished in a pit of misery, and he just told the truth. But he swore to the boy that he would never let him down; he had brought him to the hall, and he would leave him to inherit, even though he had his own boy to think of."

"Poor Philip," Clarissa said sadly.

"Do not waste too many tears on that young man. He was cruel and hateful even before he found out who he was. It's just in him, Miss. I wouldn't cross that man willingly."

"Indeed. Well, I suppose I now know why my own brother despised me and still does," Felix said and felt a curious relief; the truth was ugly, but he realised it was always a thing worth having.

"Poor Lucy had a stroke the following day, and then all those infections which almost killed her. But I do not reckon it was either one of those things which stole her mind; it was the way Philip had spoken to her, telling her blood made no difference, a lowly servant who did not have the self-respect to wait for marriage was never going to be a mother to him. It finished her, that did. Poor Lucy was never the same again. And to think he knows she's out there, living in that cottage with that bloody awful woman, Marjorie Ames! How can he sit in that grand house and know that his own mother lives out there in the grounds? No, Miss, do not waste your tears on that man. And do not turn your back on him either, he is as mean and as devious as they come."

By the time they left Francis Carlson, the man was in good spirits. It was as if he had purged himself, he had finally let go of the burden he had carried for so long. He had agreed that he would speak when the time came, and he would not hide what he had done for his master.

"I have a hankering to call upon Lucy, Clarissa. Would you care to come with me? I am sure she would be pleased to see you."

"Yes, I would like that very much. We will have to walk around the edge of the estate though, Felix, if we are to keep to the shadows, as it were."

"You are really rather good at all this, are not you?" he said, feeling a swell of admiration.

As they continued to walk side-by-side, deeper and deeper into the woodland, Felix had to fight an almost overwhelming urge to take her into his arms again and kiss her. But how could he do so when he had claimed he would never do that again? He had declared himself to be a gentleman, but he was not entirely sure he was that exactly.

"I think all of this is drawing to a conclusion, one way or another. I think we might have to wait it out a while yet, though, until we have a clear way forward in terms of the smuggling and what have you," Clarissa chattered happily as if this was everyday conversation; the stuff of polite drawing rooms up and down the country.

He tried to imagine fine ladies rattling their teacups and declaring that they really must do something about the smuggling situation. It was ridiculous, and he was certain that nobody other than Clarissa Tate could make such daring talk sound normal.

When they were finally on the other side of the estate, almost an hour later, Felix felt his spirit lifting. If things were to change, perhaps he really could do something for Lucy now. His first task would, of course, be to jettison that dreadful Marjorie Ames.

"Felix, stop," Clarissa said in a hiss, taking his arm firmly and leading him behind a thick growth of hawthorn.

"What is it?" he said, seeing a look of utter confusion on her face.

"Look, Marjorie Ames is bidding somebody farewell," she said, and he followed her gaze to the garden gate where Marjorie was, indeed, in conversation with a man. "And I know him," she went on, her brow furrowed, and her head tilted to one side.

"Oh no, surely it is not your pasty-faced suitor?"

"Fine perception, Felix, for it is the very same."

Chapter Twenty-Six

Clarissa felt that she was in stasis once more. She and Felix had again agreed not to meet for some days whilst his attorney was set to some enquiries in Bodmin to ascertain a little background on the pasty-faced, long-necked Daniel Morgan. Every time Clarissa thought she had all of the pieces of the puzzle, it seemed that another one appeared, and she must find some way to make it fit. Well, Daniel Morgan was now that puzzle piece and she would not rest until they had an answer of some kind.

All of this was tied together somehow; the smuggling, and the current earl's certain knowledge that he was not, in fact, Philip Ravenswood, but rather Arnold Bates. Arnold Bates, son of Lucy Bates, his nurse. But what was Daniel Morgan to do with it all? How did a man of his class from Bodmin come to be acquainted with Marjorie Ames, a woman who had worked as a servant all her life at Northcott Hall? It did not make sense, and Clarissa was becoming slowly exhausted.

She had, however, given herself entirely over to rest for two whole days, with no more searching through her guardian's diaries, no more mystery to uncover in order to allow the man she loved to live in peace. Instead, she had enjoyed a hot bath, some hearty meals, and many hours laying on her bed in her chamber reading romantic novels.

Clarissa was slowly finding her energy again, making the best use of the calm before the storm; for Clarissa knew, deep down, that a storm was coming.

On her third day without Felix, Clarissa had been about to retire for the night when she realised that the novel which she had been reading had but pages left to go. She decided to collect another from the library, to have it on her bedside table just in case she could not sleep immediately.

And so, she wandered down the stairs to choose a book before she dressed for bed. The main entrance hall was deserted, and she could hear no sound of chatter coming from the drawing room. She had eaten dinner with Philip and Eliza earlier, maintaining her appearance of acquiescence and pristine manners, finding herself relieved to finally be away from them. Perhaps they had retired too, although it was a little early for them, she knew.

As Clarissa walked down the corridor towards the library, she heard muted conversation. Seeing the door to the Earl's study very slightly ajar, she knew the sound was coming from there. She crept a little closer to it, listening intently, and could hear the sound of two men talking inside, one of them quite clearly Philip.

Who would have called at that time of night to speak to the Earl in private? She had an awful feeling that it was Captain Boscowan, and she listened all the more intently.

"And you are sure of this, are you?" Philip said, as Clarissa held her breath, knowing that she would have no chance of escape if they suddenly left the room.

"You must not worry about it, Lord Northcott, it is as good as dealt with." The voice was oddly clipped, that peculiar strained upper-class tone of none other than Daniel Morgan. "I have a man who is already making his way to Captain Boscowan now. He will point him in the direction of Smugglers' Cove; he is probably even giving him the information as we speak."

"Yes, but you have *everything* in place at Smugglers Cove?" Philip sounded intent, his voice far from a whisper, as usual.

"I have a small group coming into Smugglers' Cove tonight. And they have no idea that there will be soldiers there to catch them in the act."

"You are sure they will not suspect? They will not give you away and, by turn, give me away?"

"It is done, it is as good as done. Our sacrificial lambs on the little wooden gig at the Cove will have no idea they have been betrayed. They will simply think they have been dreadfully unlucky to be happened upon by the Militia; it is perfect. And there is no way that Captain Boscowan will not link Felix Ravenswood to it all, for how could the association possibly be escaped? The man's own cove, for God's sake!" Daniel gave that awful, braying laugh. "Meanwhile, the real consignment will come in at Polridmouth Cove on the other side of the peninsula!" he said triumphantly.

"And with the soldiers suitably distracted at Smugglers' Cove, our biggest haul yet can come up without interference. We will be killing two birds with one stone." Philip laughed and Clarissa was reminded of Francis Carlson's words, *"Never turn your back on him."*

Clarissa knew she must do something and do it immediately. She tip-toed away; she did not need to hear any more.

Clarissa did not even stop to take a shawl or a cloak, she simply slipped out of the front door of Northcott and darted away into the night in her short-sleeved, lightweight gown. She ran across the lawns as if the very Devil himself were chasing her, giving little thought to the idea that she might be seen tearing through the estate in a pale blue gown in the darkness. She had to get to him, and that was all there was to it. She had to intercept the soldiers and tell them what was really happening.

By the time she reached the edge of the estate, she was breathing hard. Clarissa had never run so hard in her life and she knew that she still had more than a mile to go. She gripped the skirt of her gown with both hands, raising it high enough that she might run freely and not fall. She could not stop now, even though the rain began to fall, and she could feel the sharp wind coming in off the sea and tearing across the undulating ground of the Gribben Peninsula. Even with her heart pounding in her ears, Clarissa could hear the waves in the distance crashing onto the rocks and knew that this was a characteristically rough Cornish night. With every step, the rain seemed to fall harder and harder until her hair, which was already breaking free of its moorings, was wet and clinging to her neck.

When she reached the top of the steep pathway down into Smugglers' Cove, Clarissa knew that something was already wrong. She could hear shouts, even screams, and she ran hard down that slope, losing her footing and toppling forward, grazing her hands as she landed.

Having no time to recover herself, she jumped to her feet and continued to run, just about able to see her way clear by the light of the moon. Felix was already on the cove and staring out in dismay when she arrived.

"We need help, they have run into the rocks," he said, looking at her, the full horror of the situation dawning on him.

"They are smugglers, Felix, and they have been sent here by Philip and Daniel Morgan."

"It does not matter who sent them here, not yet. Look, the boat is breaking up and they will drown, those of them who cannot swim," he said and began to run forward.

So far one man was in trouble, having clearly been pitched from the little wooden gig the moment the vessel had been slammed into the rocks by the rough sea. He was crying out, his cries seeming gargled every time the cold saltwater found its way into his mouth.

Felix ran, splashing through the waves and finally throwing himself into the water, swimming out towards the man. Clarissa could see the other men, two of them swimming confidently to shore, another one clinging desperately to what was left of the wooden gig as the long oars floated away.

Hearing shouts and footsteps coming down into the cove, Clarissa knew that the soldiers had arrived.

Chapter Twenty-Seven

No sooner had Felix pulled the spluttering man to the shore than they were surrounded by soldiers. Felix was roughly seized, two soldiers either side of him gripping his arms tightly. Other soldiers had tackled the two men who had got to shore and were trying to escape.

"Stop! Please stop! This is a trap, for goodness sake!" Clarissa yelled, trying to make her voice heard over the howling wind and the crashing sea, not to mention the shouts of the soldiers. "Where is Captain Boscowan? I must see him!"

Her arm was suddenly taken, but not roughly, and she turned to see that it was Captain Boscowan himself, looking down at her with some disappointment.

"Miss Tate, I never thought to see you here," he said, as if it truly pained him.

"Captain, this is a trap. You must listen to me. This is not Felix's fault; he is not a smuggler. You have to send your soldiers to Polridmouth Cove, that is where the largest consignment of contraband is coming in tonight. It is coming in now," she said, beginning to feel frustrated and feeling that frustration turn into tears; he was *not* listening.

"Perhaps I should be hearing this from you, sir," he said, striding away from her to where Felix was held.

"All I can tell you, Captain, is that this is *not* my doing. I heard shouts down on the cove and came out of my house to find these men struggling, their boat dashed on the rocks. I had just arrived when Miss Tate appeared, trying to warn me of something. But, like you, I did not listen, but only because I could see a man beginning to drown. All I can do is profess my innocence, nothing more," he said, breathing hard, soaking wet, and clearly exhausted.

As the men continued to talk, Clarissa could see that the man who had been clinging to the remains of the wooden gig had now been set adrift and, worse still, he was not a man, but a boy.

She ran back down to the shore, turning in the darkness and imagining that somebody would at least be following her. She called back, yelling for help, but the wind stole her voice the moment it came from her mouth and blew it inland, far over their heads.

The boy was struggling for all he was worth, but it was very clear to her that he could not swim. He was so close to the shore; she knew it would be an awful thing for him to drown within reach of safety. With nothing else for it, she began to wade into the water, its icy coldness such a shock that she cried out again. Clarissa had not swum since she was a child and she could not be certain that she still remembered how. But as soon as she was out of her depth, she began to claw at the water, stroke after stroke, just as she had done when her father had taught all those years ago, determined that his only child should always know how to save herself.

The pull of the tide was awful, and she struck out towards a rock, the faint moonlight gleaming in its black glassy surface. She reached out a hand and clung to a sharp edge, searching that inky dark water for any sign of the boy. By some miracle, he appeared, his sodden pale hair emerging from the water as he made a last-ditch effort to save his own life. Still clinging to the rock, she stretched suddenly, grasping and grasping until she found the collar of his smock shirt.

She was exhausted, pulling him towards her and having him cling to the rock as well as he could manage.

She looked miserably towards the shore, still having one hand on the rock and one hand on the boy, lest he let go in his exhaustion and drown at last. In the pale light she could see the commotion in that virgin sand, Felix breaking free from his captors and pounding away from them, down to the water's edge; he had seen, and he was coming for her.

As he swam strongly towards her, she realised that another man followed. When Felix reached her, he tried to have her let go of the boy, but she would not.

"I have him, Miss Tate, let him go." Suddenly the other man was there, a soldier; Captain Boscowan.

The short journey to the shore was something that Clarissa would never forget. Both she and the boy were pulled free, set down on the sand, soaking, shaking, unable to believe that they had come out of it alive.

"Clarissa," Felix said, dropping to his knees in front of her, reaching out for her even as two soldiers came to recapture their prisoner.

"Leave him!" Captain Boscowan said roughly, stopping his men in their tracks before peering down at Clarissa.

"You do go to some lengths to have me listen to you, Miss Tate, I will give you that," he said, those wonderful gentle Cornish tones soothing her, making her suddenly believe that everything really would be all right. "So, now you have my attention, young lady, say what you must say."

Clarissa told her story as quickly and as accurately as she could. The Captain listened, nodding, a look of recognition in his eyes and she realised then that he, that great judge of character, had likely sensed a little something wrong with both Philip Ravenswood and Daniel Morgan before. There was a look on his face which suggested the pieces were finally falling into place for him too, and she was greatly relieved to see it.

The soldiers, led by Captain Boscowan, soon cleared the cove, making their way to the other side of the peninsular at speed. Although it was clear that the Captain believed that Felix Ravenswood truly had been falsely suspected, he left a soldier standing guard outside Farwynnen House in case he was proved wrong and the man took to his heels.

"Sit by the fire, Clarissa. Oh, how I wish that Bess was here!" he said, strangely wild and excited when he led her into the warmth and safety of the house. "I must find cloths to dry us with. No; you must have dry clothes," he said, shaking his head. "Where am I to find a gown for you?"

"Felix, Felix!" Clarissa said and began to laugh. "Felix it does not matter. Do you not see it is done now? It is finished, and all we need do is hand over everything we have and leave the rest to the authorities. There is nothing left for us to do."

"Perhaps one of my nightshirts, that would do it," he said, as if he had not heard her at all.

"Felix, are you listening?" she said, walking away from the fireside to stand before him.

"I am trying to take my mind off the fact that I am, for the second time in our short friendship, so furious with you that I can hardly concentrate," he said, and Clarissa had a feeling she knew what was coming.

"Felix, nobody was listening. I could see that boy was drowning and I could not leave him."

"I know, I know. God knows, if you had not come here this night, I would already be on my way to Dartmoor prison, I have no doubt. I just wish that you could manage these things without leading me to the point of almost losing you, because I cannot bear it." He seized her shoulders, just as he had done that night in the cave, and pulled her towards him. He kissed her with determination and passion, and she immediately wrapped her arms around his neck, determined to hold fast to him this time if he should try to draw away. But he did not, he kept kissing and kissing her, his arms around her waist, pulling her body hard up against his own.

In the end, they broke apart naturally, breathless, exhausted, excited.

"I won't be a moment," he said, shaking his head violently and starting to walk out of the room.

"Where are you going?" she called after him.

"I am going to fetch that soldier in here out of the rain," he said and paused, turning to look at her. "For your sake rather than his, because with him in the house, I must be a gentleman."

Chapter Twenty-Eight

"None of it seems possible to me," Bess Pengelly's voice drifted through the house to greet Clarissa as she finally came downstairs.

She was still wearing Felix's nightshirt, with his thick long dressing gown belted about her waist. She felt awkward, coming down in such a fashion, but she had wanted to know what the day would bring. Having no idea what the time was, she guessed it was nearer to midday than morning.

Clarissa had slept in Felix's bed, whilst Felix had kept downstairs with the soldier keeping guard, ensuring Felix's continued gentlemanly behaviour. Clarissa could hear Felix's voice too, realising that he was surely in that great long room which served as both sitting room and dining room. She tentatively made her way in as Bess continued to talk.

Oh, but if you are pulling my leg, sir, if you are pulling my leg…" She left her humorous threat hanging in the air.

"I swear it to you, Bess. Bless me, you are a suspicious woman!" Felix barked a laugh, and Clarissa smiled to herself.

Felix Ravenswood and Bess Pengelly made rather a pair and she was certain that two more like them could not be found in all of Cornwall.

"I have learned to be a suspicious woman, sir. *My Lord*; oh, this is too much. Really, you were *sir* yesterday, *My Lord* today; who will you be tomorrow? *Your Majesty?*" Bess sounded excited and scandalised all at once, and Clarissa could not help but laugh.

"Ah, there she is," Bess was on her feet and hastening towards her. "Now you come and sit by the fire. *His Lordship*," she said, with heavy emphasis on the title, "told me it was too warm a day for a fire, but I said *no*, not with a lady in the house. Not after everything that poor child went through last night! Now settle down here, and I will see about a nice cup of my strongest tea for you." And with that, she bustled away.

"Felix, good morning."

"Good *afternoon*, Clarissa," he said with a grin.

"Have I really slept for so long? I did not stir at all, not once."

"Good, after these last few months, nobody deserves a rest better than you do."

"That is kind of you, *Your Majesty*, but I wonder if you might do something about my mode of dress. I cannot make a move in this nightshirt and dressing gown, it is unseemly."

"*Your Majesty,* indeed! " He grinned. "How am I going to claw my way through life now with you on one side and Bess Pengelly on the other?" He rose from his armchair to sit beside her on the couch.

"Your life? You mean you do want me in your life now that this is almost over?" she said cautiously.

"Of course, I want you in my life, Clarissa. I love you. I think I fell in love with you the very first day. Who could not fall in love with a woman brave enough to make her way to Smuggler' Cove to help a man she had never met?"

"You do not know what it means to me to hear you say that, Felix. I have loved you for so long and I have been so afraid that you would never feel the same way."

"I tried not feel the same way, Clarissa, God knows I did. I knew you were special, from the very beginning. I knew you had a tender heart and I knew that heart would feel everything deeply. Love, pain, regret. I was determined not to hurt you; I tried to keep you at arm's length in my own way. I do not think that worked very well, if I am entirely honest," he said, finishing on a humorous note.

"Well, we all have our talents," Clarissa shrugged, and he laughed, taking her hands in his own.

"Well, you cannot go back to Northcott Hall now, can you? And you cannot stay here without the benefit of the Lord's blessing. So, what are we to do?"

"What are you saying?"

"I am asking you to marry me, Clarissa. I am asking you to be my wife and stay with me forever. When I saw you plunge into that water, risking your life for a second time, I knew it would destroy me to ever lose you. I knew the time had come to give into my feelings, to let happiness come to me in a way that I have not done before. I realise now that I am more like my father than I would ever care to admit, and I understand what it is to be afraid to live, to be happy. But I will not make the mistakes he made; I will learn from them instead. It is the only way to have peace now, but I must have you in my life. I must."

"Of course, I will marry you, Felix. Of course, I will spend the rest of my life with you. I love you so much."

"And I love you. I will always love you."

Epilogue

"Well, I always knew you were going to be an interesting young lady, Clarissa. Did I not always tell you what a good judge of character I am?" Lady Gwendolyn Marchmont said, staring out across the long lawn of Northcott Hall.

"If you do say so yourself, Gwen," Felix said, walking out through the morning room doors to join them on the terrace.

"Well, I am glad not to have disappointed you, Gwen." Clarissa laughed.

"I should say not. Goodness, what a year! The old Earl passes away, you sneak this young man into his own home, you dodge a dreadful marriage to the oily Daniel Morgan, explode a smuggling ring, and then marry the man of your dreams. Oh yes, you uncover a deeply buried family secret, and find yourself expecting your first child when you have been married but three months. Am I missing anything?"

"I must admit, Gwen, that I had never expected my life to be so crowded with incidents," Clarissa said seriously, and Felix and Gwen both laughed.

Everything really had happened so quickly. On that wonderful day on which Felix had proposed to her, Captain Boscowan and the local magistrate had appeared at Farwynnen House to tell them that Felix was clear of suspicion.

The smugglers had been apprehended at Polridmouth Cove the night before, and they had been quickly persuaded to own up to the fact they were taking the contraband to Northcott Hall. Soldiers had immediately made their way there, detaining the man they thought was the Earl, and his companion, Daniel Morgan. A thorough search had discovered the hide; a hatch into a cellar below, the door of which had been disguised with a rug and a little furniture on top of it. But the soldiers had quickly removed all of that, opened the hatch with the squeaking hinge, and discovered enough tobacco, lace, and silk within to declare it to be a genuine smuggler's hide.

Any sensibilities the magistrate was suffering when it came to thoroughly prosecuting Philip had been dissolved when Felix had provided the evidence necessary to prove that the man was actually Arnold Bates, son of Lucy Bates. He was not an earl after all, and the magistrate saw fit to prosecute him.

Arnold Bates had immediately turned on Daniel Morgan, claiming that he had been forced into criminality as a result of his relentless blackmailing. Felix's own attorney had been able to add to the mounting evidence, having completed his own investigations in Bodmin which Felix had previously set him to.

Daniel Morgan was Marjorie Ames' nephew; the son of her younger sister. He had clawed his way from near poverty to affluence with his determination and skill in organising desperate smugglers. With his affluence had come great dreams of climbing out of his class, and Clarissa had not been at all surprised to discover that those awful clipped tones were nothing more than an attempt to disguise a broad Cornish accent.

His growing wealth and his move to Tywardreath had made him dream of being another man altogether, even having designs on taking a wife of some breeding. And Clarissa Tate, ward of the old earl and the daughter of a baronet would do very nicely. And so, when his devious aunt had told him every detail that she had managed to slowly extract from Lucy Bates over the years, he turned his hand to blackmail. But he did not want money, he wanted a fine wife. And in finding Arthur Bates to be so determined to keep his secret and to continue to have the world believe that he was the true Earl of Northcott, Daniel Morgan had found easy prey. It was a simple step to have the man turn over Northcott Hall as a smuggler's hide.

"Talking of incidents, I take it you have heard the sentencing handed down from the Court of the Assizes?" Gwen went on, her eyes bright with excitement.

"Yes, although I do not like to think of a young man hanging," Clarissa said genuinely.

"Daniel Morgan had hurt many over the years; lives were lost on his long road to affluence. They could have passed no other sentence." Felix sat down beside her and took her hand.

"I believe Marjory Ames has moved away to Bodmin to escape all the furore," Gwen continued.

"Yes, and she is no great loss. Finally, dear Lucy has someone kind to help her though her days." Felix smiled; his old nurse meant so much to him.

It had come as no surprise to Clarissa that Felix had moved Bess Pengelly and her husband into retirement cottages on the estate. It was pure genius, however, which had seen him move them into the cottage nearest to Lucy, so that Bess might take on a new role of caring for her. Clarissa knew that her tender-hearted husband, a man she had once thought so rough and isolated, wanted to keep both of those dear women close to him and safe.

"And at least Philip, or should I say *Arnold Bates*, did not hang." Gwen turned to Felix. "I do not think you could have stood it, my dear."

"No, I could not. The Judge took his curious life and circumstances into account, declaring that he had been put under terrible pressure to commit his crime. It is enough that his prison sentence will shock him, and his circumstances will be reduced when he is freed; he will not live in luxury again."

"Oh yes, they are to live in a little house Eliza's father has found for them. Oh, to be a fly on the wall. Imagine how sour she looks now. No title, no estate, and a husband called Arnold!" Gwen burst out laughing.

"I would still never turn my back on him, but I think he is now a toothless tiger, so to speak." Felix nodded.

Clarissa had been relieved that Arnold Bates had not hung. She knew that it would have been another care to steal her husband's peace; the peace he had only just won from the discovery of his father's secret. It was enough for Felix that Arnold was punished. It was enough for him that they had been able to give his real brother a proper burial at last. He was not a man who needed revenge, and he was not a man who could not find a little understanding in his heart.

"Well, Lady Northcott, it is time I took my leave. My husband will be wondering where I am," Gwen said and rose from her seat.

"Oh, I still cannot get used to it. I hear *Lady Northcott* and I think of Eliza." Clarissa winced.

"You will get past it. And you will make a much better Countess than she ever could."

When Gwen had gone, Felix and Clarissa sat in the garden, enjoying the last of the sunshine.

"You really do make a wonderful Countess," he said, reaching over from his garden seat to take his wife's hand.

"And you make a wonderful Earl," she said, turning to look into his eyes, watching as that unruly hair lifted on the breeze. "Such a handsome one."

"That is very romantic, my love."

"I am feeling romantic today."

"Then let us go to Farwynnen and watch the sun go down from the arched windows. What do you say? Are you too grand to spend a night there now?"

"I shall never be too grand to spend a night in the most beautiful place on earth."

The End

ABOUT THE AUTHOR

Kate Carteret was born in Bedfordshire, UK, but has lived all over the country. A freelance fiction ghostwriter by trade, Kate has now published several of her own titles on Amazon, predominantly in eBook format.

Look out for more Kate Carteret titles on Amazon.

NOTE FROM THE AUTHOR

Thank you so much for reading my book. I hope you enjoyed reading it as much as I enjoyed writing it.
As an independent author, I rely on customer reviews on Amazon and it would mean a great deal to me to read your own honest opinions of my book.

For updates on new book releases, please follow my author page on Amazon. Join me on Facebook at **www.facebook.com/DashingDandies.com**

I'd love to hear from you!

Kate

Printed in Great Britain
by Amazon

39488206R00108